Overshadowed

Until the Day Break
The Street Singer
Through Golden Meadows
The Queen's Jest
By Strange Paths
Riven Fetters
Unto the Uttermost
The Substitute
The Torchbearer
The Wayward Heart
The Thunderbolt
The Bond Slave
The Barrier
The Silver Cord
Ginger
The Long Search
The Snare
The Last Surrender
The Hidden Treasure
Beyond the Shadows
The Shattered Wall
The Singing Angel
Romance Along the Bayou
Light From the Hill
At the Crossroads
Interrupted Melody
The Scar
The Love That Lingered
The Trail
The Secret Conflict
The Promise
The Last Cry
Down a Dark Road

Overshadowed

by

Sallie Lee Bell

ZONDERVAN PUBLISHING HOUSE
Grand Rapids   Michigan

Printed in the United States of America

Overshadowed

CHAPTER ONE

DAVID WARNER SAT ALONE in the dusk of a summer evening. About him birds twittered softly as they sought their familiar resting places for the night. Blown by the gentle breeze, the scent of roses floated toward him. A butterfly flew lazily across the lawn to rest for a moment upon the edge of a lily, as if uncertain whether to resume its search for hidden honey or give up and seek a hiding place and the folding of its lovely patterned wings.

The family had gone to a concert in one of the nearby schools, sponsored by the parent teachers' association. David's mother had tried to persuade him to go, but he had begged to stay at home. He'd had enough embarrassment for one day and he was in no mood to run the risk of more.

His father had just given him one cold glance, but said nothing as he joined his mother and sister and left with them. Now David sat moody and dejected, hurt once more by that glance as well as his father's indifference. He had grown accustomed to his father's coldness, except when he reprimanded David for something he had done to displease him. It seemed that David was always displeasing his father.

At the time of David's birth, his father had been bursting with pride when he knew that the baby was a boy. He could scarcely contain his joy. Even though the little mite that was his son was unusually red and wrinkled and was not a pretty baby by any means, Mr. Warner was rejoicing and didn't let that little detail mar his joy. Little babies were generally not too lovely at birth, he knew. He was eager to show his son to kind friends and neighbors who came in to take a look, as soon as his wife and the baby returned from the hospital.

He received his first rude shock when a visitor made a thoughtless and unkind remark.

7

"My! What a funny looking little fellow!" she said when she got her first look.

She realized her blunder and hastened to cover up her stupidity.

"But most little babies look a sight when they're so young. I know he'll grow better looking every day and before long he'll be looking like his handsome daddy."

Edward stood looking down at his son without replying. He wondered if that could ever be possible. He had his doubts, for only a miracle could make his child look anything but terribly homely. His son was about the homeliest baby, to put it mildly, he had ever seen.

After the woman left, he returned to his wife's bedside and stood looking down at his sleeping son. What cruel twist of fate had given him a child like this? The baby's features seemed out of proportion. The mouth looked twice as large as it should be, and his ears were so large that they made him look like some comic book caricature. The little nose had an unfinished look, as if it hadn't completed growing.

Bitterness filled his soul as he stood looking down at the child. What kind of a trick was this that God had played on him? Instead of giving him a normal boy, He had sent some human monster of whom he would always be ashamed. Edward turned away. He was thankful that his wife had gone to sleep as soon as the guest had left.

But his wife hadn't gone to sleep. She had seen the expression upon her husband's face and in his eyes, and she had closed her eyes so that she might not have to meet his stricken gaze when he returned.

He stood there so long gazing down at their child that she thought he had gone and she opened her eyes. It was a shock to see the expression on his face as he looked down at the sleeping baby.

"Oh! Ed, darling, don't look like that!" she cried. "You look as if you had hatred in your heart. Don't look like that. Little David can't help it because he's not a pretty baby. Don't hate him!"

"I'm not hating him. I'm not blaming him. I'm blaming God for doing such a thing to us!" he cried bitterly. "I — I —"

"Don't say it, Edward!" she cried. "Don't you dare blame

God! You wanted a son and He's given you one, so just make the best of it and try to be grateful."

"Grateful! Grateful for that!" he cried wrathfully. "I wish he'd never been born!"

"How can you say such a thing! You're sinning against God! No matter what our baby looks like, he's ours and I love him and I know that one day you'll be proud to call him son. I know I shall be. God has something in life for him, no matter if he isn't beautiful now. I've prayed too hard and too often that this would be true and I'm not going to doubt God now."

"You can believe what you want to, but I'm through. I'll never have any feeling but shame, and there is no love in my heart for him. Neither can there be any love in my heart for God after this."

"You'll regret those words some day, Edward Warner, believe me, you will. And I'll be there to tell you, 'I told you so.'" Her lips trembled as tears slowly rolled down her pale face.

He leaned over and wiped the tears away, planting a kiss upon her cheek.

"I didn't mean to hurt you," he said tenderly. "Forgive me. But I'm so disappointed. I was hoping the baby would look like you, if it was a girl, for you're so beautiful."

"And I was hoping that he would look like you," she whispered as she reached up and touched his cheek.

"And look what we got!" he cried as a sob tore itself from his throat.

He turned away and left the room as his wife put her arm around the tiny baby and held him close. She murmured into that ear that was so out of proportion, "No matter what anyone thinks of you, you're beautiful to me and I love you. I love you!" She pressed a kiss on the soft baby cheek that was still red and wrinkled, though it should have been smooth and pink.

As time passed little David grew strong and sturdy and his sunny laughing disposition won the growing love of his mother as it attracted those who knew him. His little body was perfect and he learned to walk long before other babies of his age usually learned. And he showed other skills remarkable in one so young. Proud of his accomplishments, his mother knew he had a good mind that would mean so much to him when he grew older.

But when strangers saw David for the first time, they had to repress a remark that almost burst from their lips. "What a homely child!"

While David was still a small child and remained at home, there was not a cloud in his little world. Only sunshine and happiness surrounded him, for his mother lavished love and tenderness upon him. He was not old enough to observe his father's indifference.

And he was too young to be jealous of his little sister who had come along a few years later. She was such a beautiful baby that everyone remarked about her loveliness.

It was when he first started to Sunday school that David was made aware that all his world was not sunshine and happiness. When other children who were a little older than he saw him for the first time, they either stared at him with wide eyes or started giggling.

One little child, somewhat older and more outspoken than the others, stared at him silently for a long time when David first came in, then cried, "You're so ugly. Why are you so ugly?"

David stood silently, his mouth sagging and his lip quivering. Two big tears rolled down his little frecked face.

"My mamma says I'm her beautiful child," he stammered through sobs.

The other children giggled while the questioner turned away and proceeded to ignore him. The sympathetic teacher came to David and wiped the tears away.

"Just don't mind what that bad little boy says," she advised. "Let's go over and put these little animals in this ark, like they went in when the Lord told them to, and we'll talk about that great flood and leave that bad little boy over there all by himself."

David was soon engrossed in pairing off the animals while the teacher explained all about the flood and how God saved Noah and commanded the animals to come to Him by pairs into the ark. What a great miracle it was that God performed that day.

David was so interested in the story that he forgot his hurt. Though he didn't know what a miracle was, he knew that God was powerful.

It was much worse for David when he started regular school. Though the children in Sunday school were generally kind, because of the wisdom and kindness of the teachers, the school children were frankly brutal in their remarks about and to him. When he was at home with his mother's love and tenderness, he had always been cheerful and full of laughter and happiness. Among strangers he was timid and the unkind remarks of some of the new pupils with whom he was associated, made his first days at school, days of torture.

Lonely and hurt, he went into the corner of the playground and sat watching the others playing, until one of the teachers saw him and had pity upon him. She drew him out of his corner and called the others together.

"Now listen, you children," she began. "If you can't let David play with you, then I'll call all of you inside and make you sit out your recess period. Then you can stay after school and write a lesson on kindness."

"He doesn't want to play with us," one of them spoke up. "Just because Billy laughed at him and called him a clown, he wouldn't play with us."

"How would you like to be called a clown?" the teacher asked the one whom the child mentioned.

"I don't look like one," Billy retorted.

"You can go inside and sit down until I have a chance to talk to you," the teacher said. Then she turned to the others. "Just forget about David's looks. I don't see any beauties among you, so forget what either David looks like or what you look like. He can beat you at anything you try, I'm sure of that. He's better in his lessons than any of you. Now let him enjoy his recess with the rest of you."

That settled the matter as long as David was in that teacher's class, but it was the same problem over again in other classes as he grew older. Then he began to realize that he must be different from other children.

When he was old enough to really take stock of himself, he looked in the mirror and for the first time realized how he actually looked. The image was not a pretty one. He saw a mouth that was still too large for his face, ears that seemed enormous as he remembered the ears of other children. His face seemed all out of proportion. David remembered the boy who had called him a clown and he realized that the boy was correct. He did look like a clown. A sob escaped him as he turned away from the mirror and dropped dejectedly into a chair.

His sister Carrie was just coming in as he gazed out of the window and he really took a good look at her for the first time. He had just accepted her as she was and had never given a thought to her looks. Now he compared her to himself and the comparison was staggering. Her ears were small and her nose was just the right shape and size. Her mouth was small and her lips were curved in a lovely little line and when she smiled, she showed a row of small white teeth. His own teeth were not straight and the dentist had advised a brace, but David had been afraid of that for he didn't understand what it involved.

David had been made aware in the most cruel way that there was a difference in the appearance of people. Some were quite attractive, while others were not at all handsome. Then there was himself. He was the ugliest of them all. And with that horrible brace on his teeth, he would be even uglier than ever.

At this discovery, David was filled with gloom and bitterness. No wonder others laughed at him or looked at him as if he were some creature from a zoo.

After this inspection of himself and this revelation, David became so timid and withdrawn that he seldom took part in any of the activities of the other children. He grew moody and bitter.

As he grew older he developed another handicap. His nervousness and consciousness of his unattractive appearance, together with his father's coldness and constant fault-finding, brought on a stuttering that he couldn't control. He began to stutter and stammer even over the first word of any sentence. When he finally managed that one word, the rest came out easier, but by that time, if he was in the presence of strangers, he was paralyzed by embarrassment, not speaking unless he must.

His mother took him to their family doctor, but he gave her little hope. The problem was at the nervous center and David might overcome it as he grew older. Much to her sorrow, she realized that this was only a faint hope.

Though David knew nothing of what had happened at his birth or how his father had felt at that time, he was now old enough, at fourteen, to be unhappy and unwilling to go anywhere and to face strangers.

Tonight he sat alone thinking about himself and wondering why God had made him as he was and why there was nothing that he could do but bear it as long as he lived. Just now there was not much desire to go on living.

It was a dangerous attitude for a young boy to have, but he wasn't aware of the danger, only aware of the misery of his life and the hopelessness of it all.

CHAPTER TWO

DAVID WAS ROUSED from his unhappy reverie when the family returned. He saw his father walking up the pathway with his arm around his sister and at the sight a surge of bitterness swept through him with renewed strength. He couldn't remember a time when his father had ever shown him one little evidence of affection. Never had he made even one little gesture in that direction. If his father had ever put his arm around him, David would have been too astonished to know how to act. As a little fellow, he had often wished that his father would show him some sign of affection. As he grew older he felt that his father just tolerated him.

David had always been afraid of his father. A happy little fellow, utterly unconscious of his unattractiveness, when life was full of sunshine, he was still often fearful when he saw the expression upon his father's face. There was such cold hostility there, that though he didn't understand the meaning of that emotion, he felt it and it frightened him.

As he grew older, David knew that his father didn't love him. The feeling was instinctive even before he realized the truth. But when he realized the truth, he thought he understood the reason. He just wasn't the kind of son his father had expected him to be. It was perhaps not only because of his looks, but he was so entirely different from the boys his father admired. He cared nothing for sports and his father was an avid sports fan.

David would have loved to play on his school team, but he was so unfriendly and distant toward the boys who were first chosen, that they turned their backs on him. Even though he had excelled in his studies, the coach had yielded to their urging that he appoint someone else in David's place. David would have nothing to do with them.

David was studious for two reasons. He wanted to learn, for his studies fascinated him. Also there was the urge to excel as a student. He told himself that he could at least excel there when it seemed that everything else was denied him. The sunny disposition that he'd had as a small child gradually vanished and in its place came bitterness and resentment toward God who had made him as he was.

He didn't stop to realize that there were many people in the world who had no physical beauty, but who had overcome that handicap by making themselves not only agreeable, but helpful in life, people who had excelled in many fields.

As the family came up the steps, his sister said, "You surely missed it, Davy. The play was beautiful and Janice was wonderful. You'd have loved the way she acted her part."

"We missed you, son," his mother remarked.

His father passed him and went inside without saying anything to him and David was hurt again by that evidence of his lack of feeling.

"Come on inside and let's have some ice cream before we go to bed," his mother suggested. "I know you've been lonely, sitting here all this time."

"I don't want anything," David told her. "I'd forgotten how late it was. I have a test for tomorrow that I should have been studying for. I'd better get on up to it right now." He went slowly up the stairs while the others went into the kitchen and his mother got out the ice cream.

David was thinking of what his sister had said about Janice, how beautiful she looked and how well she acted. He was remembering the first time he had seen Janice when she had come into his class as a new pupil. Her family had moved to Cranford after school had started. Small for her age, she seemed so fragile to him, like a beautiful little flower of a girl. He thought she was the most beautiful little girl he had ever seen. That was when she was just thirteen and he had worshiped her ever since he had first met her, though he scarcely ever said a word to her.

Whenever they were together even for a brief moment, she would smile and make some remark that set his heart to wild throbbing. If her remark required an answer, he would begin to stutter and she had to leave him before he could get that first word out. Frequently she would give him a smile and a wave of her hand when there was no time even for a word, and he would remember that smile and the thrill it gave him long afterwards.

When the final examinations of that year were finished and the results were made known to the class, David had made the highest average for the year as well as the highest mark in the final examination.

The remarks of the teacher who gave out the report of the finals made him grateful, but when Janice smiled warmly and said, "Oh David! I think that was wonderful. How proud you should be because you're so smart. I wish I was half as smart as you are," he was thrilled and happy.

"Th — a — nks," he stammered while one of the boys nearby giggled.

He dreamed of her that night and from then on his one hope in life was that one day he could tell her how much he loved her and that he could hear her say that, in spite of the way he looked, she loved him. Perhaps she might love him if he could make a great name for himself and she would forget how unattractive he was.

During the remainder of his high school days David secretly worshiped her, though he seldom spoke to her because he knew that he would begin to stammer and that would be a disaster.

When it came time for college, his father decided that he should go to the state college in his home town. It would be less expensive and he had no great ambition for the boy. His mother was glad that he wouldn't have to leave home, for she knew how hard it would be for him to meet strangers among new surroundings. She told David that she was glad that she would still have him with her.

Her love and the fact that he knew she was telling the truth was small consolation for him, for he knew that his father didn't want him to go to the college he had hoped to attend, even though it offered better opportunity in the course he wanted to take. He wanted to study electronics, for he thought that would be the best opportunity he would have to make a good salary. He could never be proficient in languages, though he would have liked to prepare himself for some position in the diplomatic service — but his speech handicap would prevent him from handling that. For the same reason he knew that he could never be a teacher, not only because of his speech handicap.

For a teacher to be successful with young students, he knew that a teacher needed personality — something he had never possessed.

He was certain that Janice's parents would send her to a more exclusive college than the one he would attend, but he was almost deliriously happy when she told him she was going to attend State College.

When he tried to tell her how glad he was, he began to stammer and failed to get that first word out. As usual, she tried to help him and that made matters worse. She laughed and tried to cover up his embarrassment, for, as they grew older, she became quite adroit in handling delicate situations.

"I — I —guess I'm as glad as you are, perhaps more so," she said after a laugh. "I'm almost speechless myself. Just don't mind it if you can't say what you try to say. I know how hard it is sometimes to express ourselves."

"Th — a — nks," he said, feeling that he wanted to hide his head somewhere like an ostrich and let the world go by.

"Maybe we can help each other," she suggested. "You've said you wanted to study electronics and I want to major in languages. I know how smart you are, so perhaps you can help me with all those foreign translations."

"I — wouldn't be much help with the pronunciations," he said.

"Yes, you would," she insisted. "Getting to pronounce all those foreign words might help you to overcome your little difficulty in speech. Really, I don't mind that in the least. I like you for what you are, not for the way you talk."

"N — — N — or my looks?" he asked skeptically.

"Looks aren't everything. It's what's inside of a person that counts."

He longed to tell her that it was what was visible on the outside of her as well as her friendliness, that made her the object of his love. But he dared not, for he was afraid that if he told her that, it might end their friendship and that would indeed be a tragedy for him.

When they finally entered college, he was happy to find that he could at least make a beginning in his study of electronics and he was able to help Janice with the beginning of her study of French. He discovered that when he was engrossed in figuring out a translation, he forgot to stammer. Janice was delighted and told him so and for a moment he was so thrilled that he began to stammer and could scarcely make her understand what he was trying to say.

"Don't try to tell me," she said. "Just keep on helping me with these crazy words that mean so little to me and we'll both be happy."

He was happy until Barron Scott came along and then his whole dream world was shattered. Barron was a newcomer from the west and he was not only handsome, but he was friendly and eager to make friends. He was also a star football player and he was soon playing on the team. As usual, the girls were attracted to him because of his good looks and his prowess on the field.

Of all the girls he had met, he seemed most attracted to Janice and, to David's despair, she seemed interested in him. It was not long before they had their first date and Janice had to tell David that they couldn't have their regular evening together on Friday, because she was going to a dance with Barron.

She suggested that David should come to the dance which was open to all in the gymnasium of one of the other schools. As a little persuasion, she offered him a number of dances if he would come.

David looked at her seriously for a moment and for once he didn't stammer as he said slowly, "You know that I don't dance."

"Oh, I forgot!" she exclaimed, though she knew full well that he didn't dance, for the same reason that he didn't take part in athletics. He had told her that it was because of his speech impediment, but the real reason he never did try to dance was because that he knew that no girl would want to dance with him.

He didn't tell her the real reason why he felt as he did when he had mentioned his unattractiveness to her. Then she had told him how foolish it was for him to feel as he did about that. She reminded him that there were many other boys who were not good looking, but they had made themselves popular by their friendliness and their wit, often even laughing at themselves for being so unattractive.

He couldn't tell her why he couldn't be like that. That had been because of his father's attitude toward him. He remembered something that had happened to him in the past when he was still a small child, something that he had not quite understood at the time, but that he never forgot. When the truth gradually dawned upon him as he grew older, he did understand. With the understanding came bitterness that increased as he grew older, for it revealed to him the reason for his father's attitude toward him.

His father and mother had been talking and she was reproaching her husband for not showing more love toward his son.

"Why can't you show him a little tenderness and a little affection?" she asked.

"Because I don't feel any," he retorted.

"Do you mean to say that you have no feeling toward him?"

There was silence and David heard his father utter such a sigh that it seemed like a groan.

"It's just not natural for a father to feel that way," she said sadly. "He needs your love. He's sensitive enough already and your attitude only makes it worse for him. What hope can he have or what desire to make something of himself if you treat him even worse than you would a dog who wasn't what you expected it to be when you bought it?"

"I'd get rid of the dog," he said rather fiercely.

David heard no more, for he left the door, knowing that he shouldn't be listening. He knew just how his father felt toward him. He'd get rid of a dog that was not what he had expected it to be, but he was stuck with this son.

"Tell me what you're thinking," Janice urged as he looked so glum.

"It wouldn't be worth the telling," he said, stammering through the hurt at the memory.

CHAPTER THREE

DAVID GREW MORE UNHAPPY as time passed and he saw Janice's growing interest in Barron. They were so often together he was afraid they were in love with each other. He was not familiar with her type, that she desired to be popular with every boy she knew and that she did everything in her power to win that boy's love. She had been flattered because even such a boy as David could fall under the spell of her charm. Since nothing better offered itself at the time she was willing to appear interested in him. There was another reason — also, a selfish one. David was a brilliant scholar and she knew that he could help her with her studies and make it easier for her. In spite of his speech handicap, he had a better knowledge in translation than she had.

Her marks showed the benefit of his help. When she saw how disappointed David was because of her friendship with Barron, she felt a little guilty because she had encouraged him. But she couldn't deny herself the challenge of keeping Barron interested in her. She knew that she would be the envy of the many other girls who had hoped to "capture" the handsome newcomer.

David's mother noticed his growing despondency and she thought she knew the reason. Her heart was often burdened for him, for she knew how unhappy he was most of the time. She also knew that there was nothing she could do about it, except pray, and sometimes she confessed that her faith had its weak moments.

As a little fellow, David had gone with her to Sunday school, for he knew that he had to go and there was no argument about it. As he grew older, however, he rebelled against going and that brought on arguments and unhappiness for both of them, so she ceased to argue and gave up trying to force him to go.

When she tried to plead with him to go just to please her, he looked at her and the expression in his eyes, the one lovely feature he possessed, was so sad that tears came to her eyes.

"You know, Mom, why I don't want to go," he said slowly, speaking with difficulty. "You know how I talk and when people look at me, I know what they are thinking. It's like what I heard someone say, 'Boy! That face would stop a clock!' I just don't want to be laughed at by those people at church. It's that way with everybody I meet for the first time. I wish I was dead."

She put her arm around him and held him close. "Son, you act as if you were the homeliest person in the world. I've seen many who looked worse than you do, but they didn't seem to think about their looks. They just went on and seemed to be happy in spite of something they couldn't help. Why can't you try to be that way? If you'd only learn to trust in the Lord, He'd give you the courage and the joy you should have, no matter how you look. You'd be beautiful on the inside and, believe me, if you'd let the joy of the Lord shine through, people would see something of beauty in you."

"Joy! How could I ever know joy?" he scoffed. "Why did God let me be born? If He cared so much for me, He should know that I couldn't love Him for what He did to me."

"Don't talk like that, David," she warned. "God knew what He was doing when He made you and He knew that it was best for you to be what you are. He had a purpose in life for you and if you would be obedient to Him and trust Him to carry out that purpose in your life, you would be overshadowed by His love and you would have peace and happiness under the shadow of that love."

Just then his father came in and the conversation ended as David left the room.

"What's wrong with you two now?" he asked, for it was seldom that he ever observed anything but peace and affection between them.

"I was just trying to persuade him to go to church with me," she replied with a note of sadness.

"Why do you keep nagging him about that when you know why he won't go? What's the use of trying to make him do what he doesn't want to do? You know why he doesn't want to go."

"If you'd be a little more loving to him and if you'd set the example by going yourself, he might be persuaded to go without my arguing with him," she retorted. "You know how I pray that you'll get right with God, Ed, dear," she added tenderly.

"Let's not go over that again. We settled that long ago. Let's try to be happy in spite of everything. You be happy by doing what your conscience tells you to do and I'll try to be happy in my own way."

"I wonder if you really believe that you can be happy in your own way," she remarked.

Just then Carrie came in and looked at them with wide eyes.

"What's the battle about?" she asked as she went to her father and put her arm about him. "Is Mother trying to make a saint out of you?"

He gave her a little smile as he drew her to him. "She's having a mighty hard time trying."

"It's almost time for church," she said. "I don't suppose David will be going. I just saw him leave."

As they left, David's mother prayed silently about David.

"Lord, help me to have faith enough to keep on believing Thy Word that all things work together for good to those whom Thou hast chosen, those whom Thou dost love. Help me to rest in Thy Word about David and not to be so full of sadness because he refuses to come to Thee."

As David left the house he wandered toward a grove not far away. He sometimes went there when he was not occupied with his studies, for there he could sit and think without being interrupted. He was thinking of his mother's words. One phrase kept repeating itself over and over again. He had heard her use it so many times before. She had said that if he would trust God, he would be overshadowed by His love. Overshadowed. Just what did she mean by that? If God loved him as his mother asserted, why was he as he was? What would it be to be like other people, just ordinary looking, not actually as ugly as he was? Overshadowed. Overshadowed by God's love. He glanced up at the sky. As a little child he had been told that God lived somewhere up there in a place called heaven. He wondered what heaven looked like. Gradually a cloud drifted across the sky and slowly covered the sun which had been shining brightly, dimming its rays and also lessening the heat that had come even under the nearby trees.

"I'm overshadowed now," he said aloud in low tones.

No harmful ray from a scorching sun could touch one underneath that cloud. What did that mean where God was concerned?

Not too long before he had heard that song sung when he was still going to church. The soloist's voice was beautiful and the words and the melody thrilled him. He had forgotten the incident, but just now the memory of it returned. He sat there and began to hum the song. He remembered only a few words and just something of the melody, but presently he began to sing, "Overshadowed by His mighty love," and on with the next few words, then his voice died as he forgot the rest of the song.

Suddenly he caught his breath. He had actually been singing! And it sounded pretty good! Strange that he had never tried to sing before. He couldn't remember ever even trying to join in with the others who were singing the hymns in church. Perhaps when he was a little fellow, he might have joined the other children in their songs, but he couldn't remember. That had been before he became so conscious of his ugliness. After that consciousness had come, he had entered his world of bitterness and silence and no thought of singing had ever entered his mind.

He sang the words louder again and then he smiled. It was good. How he would love to really learn to sing. It would be a pleasure, something he could really enjoy. Then his shoulders drooped and he slumped back against the tree behind him. What good would that do? If he learned to sing, he would want to use his talent so that others might hear him and how could he ever do that? He could never face an audience. They wouldn't even want to listen to someone like him. He thought of all the singers he had seen on TV, going over them one by one in memory. Some were quite handsome, while others were just plain looking, but none of them looked as unattractive as he looked.

What was the use? Forget it! He'd just have to go on and make the best of a life that didn't seem worth living. He'd try to be a success in his chosen field of work and he'd try to make his knowledge bring him at least a little satisfaction. At least he could accomplish something that didn't depend upon physical attraction or fluent speech.

He rose and walked toward home, his shoulders drooped

with the weight of his unhappiness. He turned and looked up at the sky. The cloud was still lying across the sun.

Overshadowed, he thought. *But when the sun is overshadowed, it's gloomy down here. Overshadowed. I guess that's why I'm overshadowed and I don't like it!*

As he walked toward home, he kicked a pebble from his path and turned his back upon a sun no longer hidden behind a cloud.

CHAPTER FOUR

THOUGH JANICE WAS INTERESTED in Barron and though she had reason to believe that he was interested in her, she was not willing to let David get away from her. She knew that David worshiped at her shrine. He was a great help to her in her studies which were proving more difficult as she gave less and less time to them, busy with her conquests. She wanted to be loved and admired by every boy she knew and she did everything in her power to accomplish that.

She met David at the beginning of the week and when they met, she saw the reproach in his eyes, though he wasn't aware that he had revealed his feeling.

"I'm sorry about Friday, David," she said, "but there is so little chance for me to have some good times, that I just had to go to that dance. Could you find time to meet with me tomorrow night? I'd love to talk to you and we can study together then."

"So that I may help you with those hard problems," he replied in his slow, stammering voice.

"Now you're being mean," she replied with a pout. "You know that I like you and want your friendship, even if you don't help me with my problems. We can have a little time together and there is so little opportunity for me to have time for anything but this schedule and this heavy course that I'm taking. I wish I hadn't started it."

"I'll be there," David managed to say after he once got past that first word.

He tried to be happy in the prospect of being with her, but happiness just wouldn't come. How could he ever hope to compete with a boy like Barron who had everything that he didn't possess?

Why should a girl like Janice even bother to be friends with

25

him when he had nothing but a good mind? What did that matter to a girl when she began to look for love?

He sighed and determined that he would try to forget Janice and never even hope that she could care for him. He'd go on alone and he'd try to be willing to carry on and make the best of what he had, which seemed so little.

It was while he was in this blue mood that something happened to change the whole course of his life, although he didn't realize this until years had passed.

Betty was a slender girl, with nothing particularly attractive about her but her big blue eyes and her smile that lighted up those blue eyes and made her plain face attractive. Her smile was but a reflection of a light that glowed within her, which had lightened her pathway ever since she was a small child and had knelt one day before an altar in a children's service and dedicated her soul and her life to the Lord.

Betty's parents were consecrated Christians and they had dedicated her to the Lord before her birth. They had prayed that this child might yield her life to the Lord for whatever service He might command.

Though Betty knew nothing of this until she was old enough to understand, she had displayed an unusual interest in stories from the Bible that her grandmother would tell her. At first they were short little stories that she could understand, about a little stray lamb that the Good Shepherd went out and found and brought back to the fold, or the little fish that opened its mouth to give money to the fisherman who had to pay a tax and had no money.

When she was old enough to understand, she would ask for her favorite story. Grandmother was eager to tell it after Betty had knelt and had repeated her little prayer, "Now I lay me down to sleep. I pray the Lord my soul to keep." She didn't exactly know just then what her soul was, but if Grandmother wanted her to pray for it, it must be all right.

As she fell asleep it was to dream of the boy David who killed a mighty giant with one little stone. God had directed so that the stone sank right in the middle of that giant's forehead.

Grandmother went to be with the Lord before Betty was old enough to understand what it meant to be with the Lord in a beautiful place called heaven, but she knew that if Grandmother went there, it was where she wanted to go. Her mother carried on the teaching which the grandmother had begun, so by the time Betty was old enough to know what salvation really meant, it was simple for her to yield her heart and life to the Lord.

David met Betty one day after class when he had had an unusually difficult time with his stammering tongue. While he was struggling with that first word, one of the boys nearby uttered a wisecrack about him and the others laughed. It brought a rebuke from the teacher, who ordered the boy to leave the room.

Betty saw all this and her heart went out in sympathy for David. She had just been transferred to State and this was her first day in class.

Later she met David in the locker room as he was leaving. She gave him a smile that took away some of the gloom that weighed upon him. He thought hers the most beautiful smile he had ever seen, for, after what had happened in class, no one had even looked at him.

He tried to respond to her smile, but he knew that he failed miserably and he was even more conscious of his unattractiveness as she looked at him.

"I see that my locker is right next to yours," she remarked. "I was fortunate to get into State at all when I was so late for registration."

"Y-y — es," David managed to reply. He was still down in the depths and he didn't want to have to talk to anyone. But her lovely smile seemed to give him courage.

"I guess we'd better get acquainted," Betty continued, "Since we'll be bumping into each other so often. I'm Betty Parker. I've just moved here from Atlanta."

"I — I'm David Warner," David replied.

Her face suddenly became serious while her eyes were glowing with sympathy.

"I think that boy was terrible and I hope he gets what's coming to him. He should have more sympathy for someone who doesn't talk as glibly as he does. Some day that tongue of his will get him into trouble."

"Mine is always getting me into trouble," David stammered with a response that surprised himself.

She laughed and, after a moment's surprise at himself, he joined her.

"Don't you worry about that tongue of yours," she advised. "A slow tongue is more likely to keep its owner out of trouble than one that's too quick. Besides I'm sure that you can overcome that little impediment in your speech."

"L — l — ittle!" he cried. "It's horrible!"

"No matter. I know it can be cured. When I was a small child, I used to lisp so that people couldn't understand me. Only my precious grandmother and my mother could guess what I was trying to say. Somehow my tongue got all twisted when I tried to talk and I just formed words that never existed in the English language. But I was cured. You can see how I rattle along now," she added with a little laugh.

"H — h — how did you get cured?" he asked while a faint gleam of hope shone in his eyes.

"I'm sure that it was through the prayers of those two who loved me so much," she replied, a little glow in her eyes.

"Oh!" he breathed in disappointment.

"Don't you believe in prayer?" she asked in surprise.

He shook his head while a somber light came into his eyes. Just then the bell sounded for their next class and she got out her books hastily.

"My! How I've chattered!" she remarked. "Forgive me if I've delayed you." Then as she locked the door of her locker and slipped the key into her purse, she said, "Please don't let that boy drag you into something that both of you might be sorry for. I shall pray about you know what — even though you don't believe in prayer."

She waved to him as she hurried down the hall. He returned her wave and stood looking after her. What a difference between her and every other girl he had ever known! What a wonderful girl she was! Even though she wasn't at all pretty, there was something about her that made one forget her looks. He remembered her lovely eyes and her beautiful smile. And that sympathetic, tender voice.

No one else he had ever known had taken the trouble to be as sympathetic and as tactful as she had been. And so friendly. Others had shied away from him whenever he had tried to talk to them — or they had given him a glance that told him more plainly than words what they thought of him.

He had forgotten to be conscious of his unattractiveness while Betty had been talking with him. She had looked at him as if he was just an ordinary human with no handicap. She had treated him as if he was really good looking!

A sigh escaped him. If Janice would only look at him like that, just once. He knew that she tolerated him because of the help he gave her with her mathematics and that "crazy French," as she described it. Even so, he would always love her though he felt she would never return his love. Life once more seemed dark and hopeless and he was growing more and more tired of having to go on living it.

CHAPTER FIVE

DAVID'S GLOOM was again dispersed the next time he saw Betty. She gave him a warm smile with a word of greeting as they met on their way to a class. Janice was standing nearby talking to one of her other classmates, but she saw the greeting between the two and she gave Betty an appraising glance. She was quick to see David's eager response to the girl's greeting and that friendly smile.

Her attention was distracted for a moment from her companion and she failed to hear what the boy had said. He was making what he thought was a funny comment.

"I see you're not interested, so I'd better not take up any more of your time," he remarked and started to turn away. He was not used to being ignored in that fashion.

"I'm sorry," she hastened to apologize. "I was just wondering who that new girl is. I don't believe I've ever seen her before."

"Her name is Betty Parker. She came in late and she's making up some work. She's a friendly little person. I like her and so do the other fellows who've met her. She has such a breezy smile and she seems to want to be friends with everyone. If she's putting on an act, it's a good one."

"She probably is," she remarked with a shrug. "She certainly wouldn't win a beauty prize in a contest. I suppose that's why she seems so friendly."

The boy looked at her gravely as her claws showed beneath the lovely exterior and his brief admiration vanished.

"She doesn't seem to even be thinking about her looks. She just seems to be happy the way she is and glad to be alive."

He turned and left her and Janice knew that she had made a mistake. And she decided that she didn't like Betty Parker. She was determined that none of those who had been attracted to her should escape. Since David was one of those, she made up her mind to kill this new friendship with Betty Parker as soon as possible. David was in love with her and she wasn't willing for someone else to take him from her, even though he bored her to tears when he tried to carry on a conversation. But she still needed his help with her studies, even though she felt that she would soon be able to carry on without him. She had not yet had an admission from him that he loved her and she couldn't deny herself that little morsel that fed her vanity.

Later that day she was hoping that David would look for her as he so often did, but he was nowhere in sight. Just before she had to return to her class, she saw him walking along with Betty. Her lips drew together in a thin little line and there was fire in her eyes as she went to her class.

This class was a study in anthropology. As she took her place, she saw Betty and David enter and sit together.

The professor was teaching on the origin of the species and he went into the subject of evolution, giving as proof, the sources of many forms of lower animal life. He asked a question on the proof of the human species having been developed from the lower forms of animal life and he directed his question to Betty.

She hesitated a moment before answering while her usually cheerful expression vanished, leaving her face grave and just a little sad. Then she rose and gave the answer he had expected, perfect according to the text book as well as to his notes from a previous class.

"Good, Miss Parker," the professor remarked. He felt that he had a new student who would be a credit to his teaching.

Betty still stood and he looked at her a moment in surprise, then said, "Miss Parker, there is no need for you to stand when you answer a question, though I appreciate your desire to be courteous. You're no longer in grammar school."

Some of the students smiled and wondered what Betty would say or do, for she still stood there looking gravely at the professor.

"May I say something?" she asked quietly as her grave eyes rested on the professor.

He nodded a little impatiently, wondering what was coming and anxious to get on with the lesson.

She spoke in a quiet voice, though there was a slight tremor that disappeared as she continued. She knew that what she was going to say might bring on an explosion that would be directed against herself.

"I have answered your question according to the text book, for I do want to make a good grade here which will help me in my chosen profession, but I want you to know that I can't agree with the book, nor can I agree with what you have said about the origin of the species in regard to the origin of man."

"Just what do you mean by that?" the professor demanded with a frown. "Just why, Miss Parker, do you refuse to agree with those who possess more wisdom than you can possibly have?"

Her gaze never wavered a moment before his anger and she raised her head a little higher and looked at him with clear eyes.

"Because I don't believe it. I can't believe it, because it isn't true."

"Go on," the professor urged in icy tones. "From what source does your great knowledge come that you should dare question the veracity of greater minds than your immature one, to say nothing of my own puny intelligence?"

Someone snickered and the professor turned a warning glance in the direction of the snicker.

"I don't mean to be disrespectful, sir," she replied, "but what the text book says and what you have stated in your lecture contradicts the Bible and that is my source of information. It states that the first man was made by God Himself from the dust of the earth and therefore he couldn't have evolved from some lower form of animal life."

The professor smiled. "So you believe the Bible as it is written. That it is the infallible word of God."

"Yes, I do," she said quietly but firmly.

"Then I'm afraid you don't belong in this class, nor in fact, in this college, for greater minds than yours no longer believe that those stories in Genesis are facts. They are folk tales."

"To me, sir, every word in that Book is the word of God. I can't believe anything else, for I would deny my Lord if I did."

"You will take your seat, Miss Parker, and any further insubordination will merit your dismissal from the class."

"Oh, sir, I don't mean to be insubordinate. I shall try to

give the answers according to your lectures and the text books, but I just wanted you to know what I believe. I promise that I shall never be insubordinate."

She sat down, on the verge of tears. Some looked at her with a broad smile, while others showed sympathy in their glance, for they liked her and admired her courage in taking a stand for what she believed.

When the classes were over and those who lived in town were on their way home, David waited for her and they walked along together.

"That was a brave thing you did," he stammered as he fell in step beside her. "I never would have had the nerve to do a thing like that."

"You would have, if you had the love of God in your heart," she assured him. "I hated to seem rude and perhaps I shouldn't have done it, but the Holy Spirit seemed to tell me to get up and testify to what I believe, no matter what it cost."

"Wh — wh — what do you mean by the Holy Spirit speaking to you?" he asked.

"I'm afraid I can't explain it and I may bore you," she said hesitantly. "You see, it's like this. When a person comes to God and receives forgiveness for his sin, the Holy Spirit indwells that person and often when you have the urge to speak out and testify for the Lord or to defend His Word, it's sort of like a voice within you that gives you that urge. That is the voice of the Holy Spirit speaking to you. Then in times of temptation, He speaks to you again, warning you."

"Isn't that conscience?" David asked, stammering.

"No. There's a difference, though I can't explain it. You can't always depend upon your conscience to be your guide, for the apostle Paul says in the Bible that sometimes the conscience is seared as if by a hot iron. But you can depend upon the still small voice of the Holy Spirit if you are in the will of the Lord and want only to please Him. That's why I said what I did. I couldn't answer that question correctly and let the professor think that I believed what he was teaching. I know that he is very angry with me. But I know that from now on when I give the correct answers to questions, he'll know that I don't believe what I'm writing."

"L — l — ying, but not lying," he said with a smile.

"Perhaps, but God knows that I'm not lying, really. I don't know, though. Perhaps I'd better drop that class."

"Don't do it," he urged. "You need that course. And I'd miss you."

"Thanks. I'll think about it and pray about it. If I stay on, I'll know that I have one friend and perhaps only one."

"You have many friends," he managed to say. "You — you — you're so friendly and sweet to everyone, especially me."

"Thank you, David," she said and her warm smile lit up her face. "I try to be, because that's the way I feel toward everyone. But why did you say 'especially me'?"

"Y-o-o-u should know. My looks and my speech."

"Why should that make any difference in our friendship?" she asked in surprise. "Friends are friends, no matter what kind of a handicap either may have. As for looks, anyone can see that I'm no beauty. I used to cry about it when I saw other girls who were much prettier, but I learned later that I'm the way God made me and whatever comes to me now is for my good, that all things, even my unattractiveness, will work for good to me because the Lord has chosen me and I belong to Him. So, I'm going to be happy, though I'll never win a beauty prize, for one day I'll have a prize more wonderful when I stand before the judgment seat of Christ."

"What will that be?" he asked without stammering. He wasn't conscious of his words, just eager to hear her answer.

Her voice was low and she spoke even more slowly as her eyes grew luminous.

"I shall receive, if I'm faithful, the victor's crown and the crown of rejoicing. They're worth far more than the crown of Miss America or the crown of Miss Universe. Don't you agree?"

"I — don't know," he said slowly, haltingly. "I never knew anything about that."

"Perhaps some day I can tell you all about it," she offered as her face brightened with her smile.

"F-f-fine," he agreed, though he had his doubts that he'd ever even want to know.

What kind of victor's crown could he ever hope to win? He had no desire to win a crown, for he had no desire to be faithful to her God.

CHAPTER SIX

THOUGH MANY DAYS WERE GLOOMY for David as he struggled with his problems, time passed relentlessly. Betty's days, on the other hand, were full of joy and thanksgiving for her blessings.

After the incident when she had incurred the ire of the professor, her student life ran smoothly. She was an outstanding student and her instructors recognized something in her that the others didn't possess. She was always cheerful and never worried, even when quizz time came, because she was always prepared and didn't wait until the last minute to "cram."

She answered every question put to her by Professor Smart in the anthropology class, but when she answered the questions that didn't agree with what she believed according to her Bible, she always prefaced her remarks by little phrases, "According to the statements in the text book," or "according to the notes from your lecture."

Professor Smart couldn't fail to accept her correct answers, though her preface to the answers nettled and irritated him.

Many of the other students secretly admired her for her courage in standing for what she believed, even though they might not believe as she did. They listened to the statements she made about her belief when they asked questions about God and the Bible.

Though Betty didn't try to make herself popular, nevertheless her popularity increased as time passed and she was often asked for a date by different boys. Even though she was not pretty, and her plainness was more noticeable when she was in the same group with Janice, there was something in her expression and the light in her lovely eyes that made her more attractive than mere beauty would have done.

Janice noticed Betty's increasing popularity and was nettled by it. She treated Betty with condescending politeness, which Betty was wise enough to observe, but it didn't worry her. She was happy and grateful for the friendship that had been given her.

Betty refused some of the dates boys asked for, because she didn't dance or go to other places where they wanted to take her. Though they were surprised at her refusal, when she explained the reason for her refusal, they couldn't help but admire her for being steadfast in what she believed. She was well aware that some of the boys called her a religious fanatic, but that didn't disturb her. She remembered that the disciples had been glad that they were counted worthy to suffer shame for His name.

David enjoyed her friendship more as time passed. They were together often when the others in their group were at a dance or a cocktail party. He enjoyed their conversations, for Betty made him forget to be embarrassed when he stammered and she always had interesting subjects to talk about.

When graduation time came and David knew that he and Betty and Janice would likely be separated, he became depressed and gloomy again. The two who had meant so much to him would no longer be near at hand. He would be alone to carry on his life and he knew how lonely he would be.

Though Janice had continued to show him enough interest to keep him dangling and had given him little hints now and then that he was someone very special to her, he had never dared tell her that he loved her. He had loved her for so long that it had become a part of his life. She was present in his dreams and his hopes were built around those dreams, though he never dared voice those hopes to her.

One evening they were alone together. David rejoiced over the miracle, which was no miracle. It was a clever little scheme that Janice had managed, so that they might have a last time together.

She asked him what his future plans were and he told her that he had put in his application for a position in a major electrical plant in one of the larger cities.

"I shall miss our evenings together," she said with just the right inflection of regret. "I've loved having you for my friend, David, and I shall miss you so very much. I hope you won't forget me."

"F-f-forget you!" he exclaimed. "How could I ever forget you when I love you so!" He finished breathlessly, forgetting his fear that if he told her this, their friendship would end, forgetting everything but that he longed to take her in his arms and pour out his love to her.

She smiled, a little satisfied smile, then she said in a low soft voice, "I'm glad you love me, David, dear, for you're very dear to me. Very dear. I shall always remember you and wish that we could be together."

"D — o you mean that?" he asked eagerly, not daring to believe it, yet wishing with all his soul that he could.

"Of course I do. I wish that we didn't have to part, ever."

He looked at her a long moment, his eyes wide with surprise that changed to unbelieving joy. Then he took her in his arms and drew her close while he attempted to kiss her.

She pulled away from his lips and tried to free herself from his vicelike embrace, but she couldn't. His face drew nearer until his lips almost touched hers, then she freed one arm and gave him a resounding slap.

"How dare you presume that I'd let you kiss me, you-you-"

The next word was never uttered, for she saw the expression upon his face and in his eyes as his arms fell from her and he stood looking down at her silently.

She turned and left him, feeling suddenly ashamed, while he stood looking after her, feeling like someone who has just received a mortal wound and whose life was ebbing until he fell and lay down to die.

He finally turned and walked slowly away, without really knowing where he was going and not caring nor really seeing. And he came face to face with Betty.

He stared at her a moment without really seeing her, then he realized that it was she and he stopped and looked dully at her.

She looked into his stricken eyes with such pity and compassion that tears came into his.

"David, I'm so sorry," she said gently. "I couldn't help but see what happened, but there was no way for me to get out of sight, so I just stood here. I was coming in to get a book that I had left. She didn't even see me when she passed. Please believe that I didn't want to be an eavesdropper."

"I — believe you," he said dully. "What does it matter if you were?"

"I wish there was something that I could say to help," she murmured.

"N-n-o-thing can help. N-o-thing matters. I was just a fool to think that anyone could care for such a dud as I am."

"Please don't feel that way, David. You're not a dud and if you'd just try to believe that there are others like myself who like you and treasure your friendship, you'd be happy in spite of what one vain person has done to you."

"How can I be happy," he stammered, "when I've loved her for so long and she made me think she cared even though I am what I am? But she was just playing along with me because she knew I cared."

"You can be thankful that you have found out just what kind of a girl she is before she ruined your life. You have your whole life before you and you can make something wonderful of it, if you'll just let God take hold of it and help you. You have brains and ability and you can use them to the best advantage if you'll just try."

"I-I — don't want to try," he said as he struggled to keep back a sob.

"I know how you feel," she said and her voice was warm with sympathy. "You feel that life won't be worth living and there is no need to try to go on, but that's not true. Some day God will give you just the right girl, one who loves you for what's inside of you and not what the world sees. And you'll wonder how you could ever have been foolish enough to think that life's not worth living."

He was silent as she persisted, even though she feared he might resent her persistence.

"God loves you, even though you have never accepted His love through Christ. I'll be praying for you, that you will have every happiness life can bring you and that you will be overshadowed by His love."

He caught his breath as he stared at her and murmured slowly and stammeringly, "Overshadowed by His love. That song! I knew it long ago. Do you know it?"

"I sang it often in the choir back home. Believe it or not, I used to sing in the choir and I sang solos once in a while.

There were so few in that little church where I received my salvation."

"W — w- would you sing it for me now?" he asked. For the moment he had forgotten his shock and bitterness.

"If you'd like to hear it." Then softly, but with tones that were pure and melodious, she began to sing, "Overshadowed by His mighty love" — and on to the chorus of that beautiful, soul-stirring melody.

"Oh! Beautiful!" he breathed. "Thank you."

"I believe every word of that song," she told him. "It's been with me so many times when I've needed a little comfort or when everything seemed to go wrong. It can mean the same to you, if you'd only believe those words. You know, I think the author of that song had a certain Psalm in mind when he wrote those words. 'He shall cover thee with his feathers and under his wings shalt thou trust.'"

He shook his head. "I — I — 've tried to believe, but it doesn't work with me."

"It will some day," she stated. "God answers prayers, especially for someone's salvation. I shall be praying for you."

"Y — y — ou're a wonderful person," he said and the look that went with the words made her heart start a quicker beating.

Betty didn't know why she had fallen in love with him, but she had, almost from the beginning. She had known many others who were far more attractive and she wondered why this had happened to her. Almost from the beginning, she had known that he was in love with Janice. It was so manifest when she saw them together.

When she first met him, she had been deeply sympathetic because of his handicap and because she couldn't fail to see how unattractive he was. She saw also how unhappy and remote he was from people because of it.

Betty knew what it meant to be around others far more attractive than she was, but there was a difference. She had learned to be content in whatever situation she was, because she knew that God knew and that whatever happened to her was good for her. And she had been happy because of this trust and faith.

But now that this impossible situation had come into her life, she wondered why God had allowed it, for she knew that David never even thought of her as anyone he could fall in love with, even if he hadn't been enslaved to Janice's charm and loveliness.

She didn't want to question God's dealings with her, so she took it to Him in prayer, but as yet, she knew that her prayer had not been answered. At least He had not taken that love from her heart as she had prayed He would.

After she had left David, she went to her knees again and prayed, not only for David, that he would believe and receive the peace that could only come from God, but she prayed for herself, that this love would be taken out of her heart, if it was His will. When she rose from her knees, there was peace within her. God knew the situation and all things would work together for good to her and for David, for she believed that somehow and in some way, he would yield his life to the Lord she loved and wanted to serve. As long as she was yielded to God's will, she felt she could not fail to have peace and joy, whatever might be the answer to her prayer.

CHAPTER SEVEN

DAVID'S THOUGHTS were in confusion as he left Betty and went home. How could a girl as beautiful as Janice be so heartless and cruel. He realized now that she had only tolerated him because it satisfied her vanity. How could a man such as he satisfy any girl's vanity? She had so many other admirers, so why waste time on him?

She had used his love for her to help her when she had been either too lazy or too much occupied with other more pleasant pursuits to help herself. He was sure that she had known he was in love with her and she had deliberately led him on to do what he had done.

Hatred filled his heart as he remembered her honeyed words that had drawn out his confession and the hidden tiger within her that had prompted that slap. Memory of her look of loathing and her words of contempt brought renewed bitterness.

David wished that he could go away and, like some lover in a fairy tale, return after an absence, a hero, with everyone paying him homage. And with every girl vying for his favor or at least his recognition. Then she would be ashamed even to ask for his forgiveness for her insult.

His lip twisted in a crooked smile. How could he ever become a hero, and if he ever should become one, by some miracle, what difference would it make to her or to anyone else?

He thought of Betty. How could she be so sweet and so happy when she saw other girls much prettier, being admired by so many, when she knew that she wasn't at all pretty? What was it that made everyone like her, even though she didn't try to make them like her in the way that Janice tried? What was it that made him like her so much and enjoy being with her and why was it that every time they were together, he felt en-

41

couraged to try to go on when the going seemed so rough? Why was it that his bitterness and his humiliation seemed less after he had talked with her?

David thought of their recent conversation and he remembered how he had thrilled with delight in her lovely voice as she sang that song that he had loved long ago. She was really a wonderful person, as he had told her. She would make some fellow a wonderful wife, for she would be thinking of his happiness above everything instead of trying to keep her beauty and to be attractive to other men. And when he grew discouraged, she would have that same sweet way of giving him courage to go on, no matter what had been the cause of his gloom. There surely would be no divorce in that marriage, for she would have the ability to bring peace into whatever threatening situation might develop.

His eyes lost their hard light for a moment as he remembered how she had tried to comfort him when she had witnessed his humiliation. She had tried to make him believe that, in spite of every obstacle that came into his life, he could overcome and make his life worthwhile and happy.

He wished that what she had tried to make him believe would come true, but it would take a miracle and a great one, to make that possible. No, he couldn't believe in the kind of miracles she believed in.

God must surely have had some grudge against him to have made him what he was. How could he love God and yield his life to Him, as she had suggested? What was there to yield anyway? His life counted for nothing to anyone, except perhaps to Mom. The only thing he could hope for was to get that job and make a living and to carry on as long as he had to, and there was no hope for happiness in that outlook for his future.

His mother saw how dejected he was and her heart ached anew for him. She had seen him that way so often, for it had become his habit as he grew older. Nothing she said seemed to help. She had tried so often that it had become a habit, and he had so often listened indifferently that it had also become a habit. One thing was left to her and that had also become a habit. That was prayer and though it was a habit, it was repeated each day and night with a faith that never wavered, though sometimes she grew impatient for the answer.

"You look tired, dear," she remarked as David came in and slumped into a chair.

Though he persistently refused to yield to her plea for him to receive the salvation in which she rejoiced, he always came to her when he was down in the depths and needed love and sympathy. She was the only one, he felt, who really loved him and cared when he needed love and encouragement.

"Tell me about it," she pleaded when he only sighed and didn't answer.

"I'm not tired, I'm just disgusted with everything," he replied.

"Tell me and let me try to help you," she urged.

As a little child, he had always been eager to tell her when he was in trouble or when someone hurt him. She had always helped him to forget the hurt. But now he was no longer a child and he couldn't weep on her shoulder or in her arms and receive what little the relief of tears gave. This hurt had gone deeper than tears and he knew that even she couldn't help him. She would be hurt if he didn't tell her what had happened, he knew, and he felt that even in the telling there would be some relief. He began, however, with something that had happened before his meeting with Janice. Then he decided to let her know how he felt about that and perhaps not mention what had happened with Janice. He felt too humiliated to tell her, at least not yet.

"I'm not very happy knowing that I couldn't give that valedictory address after I'd won the honor."

He had lost sight of that first disappointment in the light of what had transpired with Janice.

"But you had the honor of being presented to the audience as the one who deserved it," she argued. "I thought it was splendid of Dr. Colt to say what he did when he presented you, telling the audience that you had been so gracious to yield your place to the one who had won second honor."

"Everyone knew why I had done such a generous thing," he replied.

"Not everyone, dear. And those who did know, understood. You should be proud of the applause they gave you. I was proud of you, very proud."

"I know, Mom," and he gave her a grateful look, "but you're the only one who'll ever be proud of me and I sometimes wonder why you care when I'm such a disappointment to you and Dad."

An ache came into her heart as it so often did when she realized how the boy felt toward his father and how his father felt toward him.

"The only disappointment you've been to me is that you never have been willing to do the one thing that would make not only me happy, but it would make you happy also."

"Please, Mom!" he cried. "Not that! I can't take it now!"

"Forgive me, son. It just slipped out," she confessed. "But what's on my heart so constantly just sort of came out before I realized it. I know that Janice must be proud of you, for I know she's grateful to you for helping her over the hard places when she was having such a time with her studies. I'm sure she must have congratulated you. She should have. Didn't she?"

"C — ongratulate me! She slapped my face!" he blurted out trying to control the sob that rose within his throat at the memory. It was out before he realized it.

"Why on earth did she do that?" she asked in astonishment.

He hesitated a moment, then, trying not to stammer, but failing utterly, "S — she m-m-ade me believe that she cared for me, in spite of what I am, but when I told her how much I loved her and tried to kiss her, she slapped me and then went away and left me. She looked at me as if I was a leper, or something as disgusting."

"Oh, I'm so sorry, son. I wish there was something that I could say, because I know how long you've loved her, but she isn't worth your love, dear. A girl like that will never make anyone happy. I feel sorry for her. She has nothing when she could have so much in life. Don't let her get you down, son. Just forget her and try to make something of your life that will make people look up to you and respect you for what you are."

"How can I forget her when I love her so much? At the same time I hate her!" he cried bitterly.

"You can set a goal for your life and work toward that goal. Try to make the best of the life that God has given you and one day you'll be glad of this experience. Believe me, you will. I know you will and I shall pray that one day the Lord will give you the one girl who is best for you, for I know that she is somewhere in this world. I have faith enough to believe that."

"I wish I had your faith," he said in hopeless voice, "but just now I don't want to do anything but try to forget my love and my hate."

"I want you to forget both and I shall pray that you will. I know that you'll succeed in that job you've applied for. One day you'll be happy, for I know that God does answer prayer."

Putting his arm around her, he gave her a feeble smile and laid his cheek against hers.

"What would I do without you, Mom?" he asked in a voice that trembled.

CHAPTER EIGHT

DAVID TRIED TO FORGET the hurt Janice had given him and he tried to forget her. But he soon realized that he couldn't. Neither could he overcome the love that he had for her and the bitterness and hate which were so mingled in his feelings toward her.

He wondered how a person could love and hate at the same time and he called himself an utter fool for having any feeling at all for her, either love or hate.

She was with him in his every waking thought and often with him in his dreams. In those dreams, he always came home famous and sought after, while throngs crowded around him just to shake his hand, while she stood at one side wanting to speak to him, yet ashamed to face him.

He had dreamed this dream so often, with many variations, that it disturbed him during his waking hours and left him in deeper gloom. His mother noticed this and worried over it, for she saw that he was retreating more and more into himself. She knew that this was a dangerous situation for anyone.

She prayed about it, but she seemed to get no solution to this problem.

On the next Sunday morning, she met Betty in church. Betty came to her just as she was leaving and stopped to speak to her.

"I want to congratulate you for the honor David received," Betty said. "I know how proud you must have been because of it. I was so proud of him and glad to be his friend."

"Thank you so much," David's mother replied. "I appreciate those words. David always speaks of you with such enthusiasm that I know how much your friendship means to him. He has so few friends. I'm sure you know the reason why."

"Yes, I understand and I've done everything I can to help

46

him believe that people want to be his friends. He has a fine mind and I'm sure that he can make his life worth-while if he'll only try."

Anne Warner smiled gently. "I'm so glad that you have won your way behind that wall he has set up between himself and the world. I know that whenever he has been with you he has a different outlook on life. I can't begin to tell you how much I appreciate what you have done for him."

"It's been a joy," Betty assured her and there was a warm light in her eyes. "I just wish I could do more. I've prayed that I might be allowed to."

"Why not come over and have dinner with us some evening soon? You name the day. We'd be so glad to have you and I know that David will be glad."

"Thank you. I shall be glad to come, but it will have to be soon, for I'll be leaving soon for a visit and then on to nurse's training."

They agreed on a day and Anne left her feeling that in some way this Christian girl might be able to do for David what she herself had been unable to do.

David was delighted when he learned that Betty was coming to dinner. He had missed her since the close of school, yet he didn't want to ask her for a date. He felt that she would only accept because she felt sorry for him and he didn't want that.

Betty proved to be a most entertaining guest. She was not a constant chatterer, but she could talk interestingly upon almost any subject and David's father was pleased and surprised when she could talk enthusiastically about fishing, one of the sports he enjoyed but which he seldom had the opportunity to pursue.

She related some of her experiences when she was a child and her father had taken her on their frequent fishing trips in his small sloop, for he loved to sail as well as fish.

"I was thrilled when I caught one now and then," she related while she smiled at the memory, "but oh, how I did hate to see my father remove the hook from that fish's mouth. I'd feel sorry for the poor thing and beg my father to put it back and let it live."

Mr. Warner smiled at her little narrative. "I'm afraid you'd never make a champion fisherman. Do you still feel that way about fish?"

"I hate to see the poor things suffer, if they really do, but I love to eat them after they're dead," she replied.

As the meal progressed, David's mother observed how much happier he seemed. He no longer sat silent and withdrawn, with that unhappy expression upon his face. His eyes glowed with interest and he joined in the laughter when Betty related some of her childhood escapades and the punishment that always followed when she deserved it.

Mrs. Warner prayed while the others talked that the Lord would use this girl to help David in a way that she never could. She asked Betty what her plans were, now that she was out of college.

"I've changed my mind about what I thought I'd like to do," Betty told her. "I had thought of going on to graduate school, so that I might be able to teach at the high school level. I thought that I might be able to help young people in their dangerous years, to live the best life there is and to counteract some of the blasphemous teachings that are handed out to them in our high schools and colleges these days. I've prayed about it and I've talked to Mother and I believe that it would be best for me to take nurse's training. I believe that I could do more with patients upon a sick bed to lead them to the Lord, than I would be able to do with students in school. I would be restrained from teaching the things that I believe. I wouldn't be free to express my belief as I attempted to do when I first attended college here. That taught me a lesson I'll never forget."

"Tell them about it," David suggested. "It was such a brave thing you did."

"Yes, do," his mother urged. "We'd like to hear it," his father added.

As briefly as she could, she related her experience in Professor Smart's class. When she had finished, there was silence for a moment.

"That was a pretty risky thing you did," Edward Warner remarked.

"It was mighty brave of you," his wife added.

"I wasn't thinking of bravery at the time, though my knees shook while I stood there. From then on Professor Smart and I lived in an unarmed truce. He had to give me good marks, for I always answered his questions correctly. I was more concerned about those questions than I was about any of my other studies, because I knew he was just hoping for an opportunity to fail me."

When the meal was over, David's mother suggested that they sit outside where it was cooler while she and his sister went into the kitchen and his father read the evening paper.

As soon as they were seated in the big swinging seat on the porch, David asked her why she had changed her plans.

"Just what I said," she replied. "I want to do the thing that may bring the greatest help to the most people. I'd love to be a missionary and if the Lord should really call me, if I was a nurse, I would have the opportunity to do so much good in the shortest possible time, even before I learned the language."

He was silent for a moment. He was thinking over what she had said. What joy could there be in nursing cranky sick people or nursing savages in some foreign land where there was so much filth and disease that was contagious? How he wished that Janice could have been just a little like this wonderful girl.

"What are your plans?" she asked, breaking the silence and wondering what his thoughts were.

"I don't have any except to get that job and make a living."

"Don't you have any real goal or any real ambition to do something definite in life? I'll repeat what I've told you before, that if you do you'll be much happier. Why not try to have some great aim, even if you never attain it? Why not try singing? You have a good voice, a good speaking voice, for it is well modulated and it has such a good quality."

"That's a good one!" he exclaimed when he finally got out that first word. "A good speaking voice when I can't even speak, just stutter and stammer. What a mess I'd make trying to sing! And who'd want to listen to me?"

She turned to him and said in severe tones, "David, you just have a fixation about your speech and your looks and it's a sin for you to feel that way about yourself. God has given you some gift and you should try to find out what it is and use it to your good and the good of others. The way you act and feel now is weakness and I don't want you to be weak. I want you to use the strength that God has given you to make the best of what you possess."

"Why should you care?" he asked in surprise, for she had never used that tone before.

"Why should I not care? I'm your friend and I know you're

mine and I'm glad of it. And because it's my desire to help others who need help. And you surely need it, for if you keep on the way you're headed, you'll end up by being a veritable old Scrooge and I'd hate that."

"What would you suggest?" he asked sarcastically. "You say that I have a good singing voice. Even if I had, who'd want to listen to a caricature like me?"

"Now you're being just what I said you were once before. You're being sorry for yourself because you're not a young Adonis. Have you ever taken a good look at yourself in the past couple of years?"

"No, I haven't," he admitted. "I hate myself every time I look into a mirror, so I don't look any more than I have to."

"Well, I've looked at you often. You know that. And maybe you haven't observed that you're much better looking than you were when I first met you. I believe that as you grow older, you'll be still better looking. But even if you're not, just think a moment of the men who have done great things in science, who've been great preachers, great doctors and I could go on naming people in every walk of life who were great, not because they had beauty of feature, but because they had the courage to give themselves to the best that was in them."

He was silent as she continued. "Some of them were pretty terrible looking. Think of Abraham Lincoln. He surely was no beauty. How many presidents were really good looking? Not too many."

"How many stammered?" he asked stammering.

"I don't know that any of them did, but many of them overcame greater handicaps. Franklin Roosevelt overcame a greater handicap than stammering. Then there was Demosthenes who did stammer. But he overcame it and became the greatest orator of his time. If he could do it, you can, too."

He was silent, for he felt rebuked and justly so. He was ashamed to admit it, but he knew that what she said was true. He had been a weakling without any ambition or aim in life. But he had no ambition to be anything better than he was, for he was steeped in self-pity.

She knew instinctively how he felt and was afraid that she had hurt him. If she had she was sorry, for he had already been deeply hurt.

She laid her hand upon his. "I didn't mean to hurt you,

David, my friend. I was just trying to help you to get out of the depths and to see that there is so much good in life for you, if you'd just try to find it and to possess it."

"I understand," he said speaking slowly so that he might not stammer on those first few words. "What would you suggest?"

"Would you let me try to teach you to sing? I'll be here a little while, after my visit, before I go on to New Orleans to enter training. If you'll come over tomorrow, I'd love to try out your voice. I've had a little training and I can help you get started. Then if you really want to learn, you might take it up to give you something to do when you get your job."

"If you think I'm worth wasting your time on, I'd love to have you for my teacher," he said as he gave her a smile that was a little more cheerful.

"Then it's agreed," she said.

Presently they heard his mother coming into the living room and they went in and joined her and his father and sister. David felt less gloomy and just a little elated as they went in.

CHAPTER NINE

THOUGH DAVID WAS AT BETTY'S ON TIME, he came with a certain feeling of uncertainty. He wasn't at all sure that he wanted to learn to sing. He wasn't at all sure that if he did learn, he would ever have the courage to face an audience. Who would want to listen to him? He remembered what Betty had told him, that if he was good enough, they would want to hear him sing, no matter what he looked like. Even if that were true, he would be afraid every time he opened his mouth that he would begin to stammer over the words of the song and ruin it completely. He was sinking back into the gloom from which his recent conversation with Betty had lifted him.

When he was with her he was inclined to agree that he had been magnifying his troubles. He realized that he should try to overcome them, but left to himself he lost the courage or the desire to do what she had endeavored to make him do. He thought that perhaps if she were always at hand to keep him encouraged, he could be what she wanted him to be, but she would soon be gone and he would not have her near and then there would be no one.

She greeted him with her usual warm smile and led the way into the living room. Her mother was there to greet him and make him feel welcome, then she left them to themselves.

"Now let's get to work," Betty suggested when they were alone. "First I want to test your voice."

She went to the piano while he stood beside her and she struck a few notes. "Now I want you to sing this note. Just say ah and try to follow me as I go up the scale."

He obeyed, but his voice was very low and weak, for he was still not relaxed and at ease.

"You're not trying very hard," she told him. "Just forget who I am and pretend that I'm a famous teacher and that you've paid a lot of money for this lesson and that you want to get your money's worth."

He laughed. "No teacher would waste time on me, even if I could pay big money for the lesson."

"There you go again, underrating yourself. If you don't try to believe in yourself and snap out of that gloomy mood, I shall be sorry that we're friends."

"Then I wouldn't have a friend in the world," he replied, his smile dying upon his lips.

"Remember what I said that the Bible said about having friends?"

He shook his head. He didn't care much what the Bible said about having friends.

"It says that for a person to have friends, he must show himself friendly. If you don't have friends, it's because you never have tried to be friendly."

He shook his head. "You're wrong. When I was a little fellow, I tried to make friends, but the kids only laughed at me. I came to hate them so that I didn't want their friendship."

"You poor fellow," she breathed. "I know how cruel children can sometimes be, but let's forget everything right now but your voice. Now put your whole soul into every sound that you utter and sing loudly, not under your breath, as if you were afraid to make a sound."

He laughed again. "That was just what I was afraid of," he stuttered.

She struck a note and sang loud and clear as she followed her fingers up the scale.

"Now you do it that way," and she struck a note.

He obeyed her instruction and his voice rang out loud and clear and mellow.

"Fine!" she cried. "I wasn't wrong. You do have a good singing voice. As soon as you learn a little about breath control and where to place your breath, down in your diaphragm and not up in your throat, you'll really surprise yourself."

He had his doubts about that, but he obeyed her and followed her through the little exercises she herself had learned years before when she had hoped to begin a singing career, before she had yielded her life completely to the Lord.

"Now let's rest for a little while and then we'll try something else," she suggested.

She led the way to a couch and invited him to sit beside her.

"You do have a very good voice," she said. "I know that you could use it in a wonderful way for the Lord, if you'd just realize what it really means to live for Him and to give all that you have of talent and resources to Him."

She saw his expression change as the light died from his eyes. The same old expression of sadness came into them.

"I know what you're going to say, even though you wouldn't want to hurt me, that you just can't feel the way I do and you're sorry. You're just not interested in anything that pertains to God or service for Him."

He was silent for she had guessed the truth at least about what he was thinking.

"Don't you realize that by having that attitude not only toward God but about yourself, that life will never mean anything to you the way it should mean?"

"I — t has never meant much to me since I realized what I was and that I lacked everything that everyone else seemed to have."

"I know. You're going through life blaming God because you didn't have the good looks that many others have — and I think that this had a large influence in making you begin to stammer. I believe that if you could overcome your bitterness toward God and your belittling of yourself, and overcome that gloom that you've wrapped yourself in, you could be a happy person. Then you'd be willing to use your talent and all that there is of you for others and for your own enjoyment. And I know that would bring happiness to you. Now let's get back to this singing lesson or you may feel I'm not earning my money."

She opened a hymn book and turned to a hymn she thought he knew.

"I'm sure you must have heard this many times when you were a little fellow and went to Sunday school," she remarked as she played it over, then sang a verse.

"Now sing a verse with me," she suggested.

He obeyed and as they sang together, he gradually let his voice ring out. Then he realized he enjoyed hearing the sound of his voice. And he liked the sound! Memory of another time when he had sung alone in that grove so long ago came to him.

She turned an eager face to him. "Did you realize something?"

He shook his head.

"You sang that whole verse without once stammering or hesitating on a single word. And you started without hesitation or a struggle to get that first word out. Don't you see? Perhaps through your singing you may overcome that stammering that has you so depressed. Then you won't have anything to keep you so unhappy."

"Except my face," and once more he stammered.

"If I were your mother, I'd take a switch to you," she said with pretended severity. "Of course both of us know that you're not handsome, but then, as I've said before, I'm no beauty either, so we're two of a kind, on the plain side of the picture. But just think of how blessed you are and don't be so bitter toward God or one day you'll be sorry, more sorry than you realize. Thank Him for your blessings. Just think of how many blessings you do have, even though you don't have what you most desire. Remember that God made you as you are and that it was for a purpose. If you believe that and thank Him for what you are, you can be just as happy in life as I am. Don't forget that I have longed for beauty, as any normal girl would. But I learned to be thankful for what I am and have. You could be thankful just as I was. You're not deformed. You have a good mind. You could be blind or crippled or insane.

"Just take a visit to the crippled children's hospital or the home for the incurables and if you don't leave there rejoicing for what you are, then I don't have much faith in you that you'll ever be anything but a grouch."

"My!" he ejaculated. "That was surely a hot sermon and it burned me up."

"I meant it to," she said with a smile. "But I did it for your good, David, not to hurt you. I'd do anything to rouse you from that discouraged state that you've fallen into, because I know that it is robbing you of so much happiness."

"I appreciate your effort, even if I can't change myself just to please you," he said, stammering.

"You can at least try," she argued as she gave him a serious, yet tender glance. "I know how much it would mean to you. How about it?"

"It might not be too difficult if you were going to be here to give me strength and encouragement."

"I shall be with you in spirit," she said playfully, then more seriously, "I shall be praying for you daily, that you may find what is best in life and the happiness that you and everyone is entitled to, if he'll only seek it from the Source of all happiness."

Just then Betty's mother came in with a tray of cake and cold drinks.

"I thought you might enjoy a little refreshment," she remarked as she set the tray down and gave David a smile.

Betty thanked her and David tried to express his thanks. Mrs. Parker appeared not to notice the struggle he was having in getting that first word out.

When she left and they had enjoyed the brief interlude David said that he should be going, that he had taken up enough of her time.

She went to the piano and played a few chords.

"Shall I sing something for you before you go?" she asked.

"I'd love it," he told her.

As her fingers ran over the keys he knew before she started to sing what the song was going to be. He listened with rapt attention as her lovely voice rang out with tender emphasis on the words of "Overshadowed."

"You remembered," he breathed when she had finished.

"I thought you'd like it," and she gave him a smile.

"I shall always remember this time and the way you sang it," he said. "And how beautiful your voice was as you sang it. That song will mean more to me than it ever did before."

"I shall be praying that one day you may be able to sing it and really let the beauty and the truth of it enter your innermost being."

At the door as she told him good-by, he took both of her hands in his and murmured, "I shall always be thankful for your friendship, for it has meant more to me than anything that ever came into my life."

"That will make me very, very happy," she replied.

If he only knew how very happy those words made her, she said to herself as she watched him until he was out of sight.

CHAPTER TEN

WHEN DAVID RETURNED from his visit with Betty, his mother saw the glow in his eyes and her hopes grew that he would fall in love with her. She was sure that Betty would be the kind of wife who would help him out of his hopelessness and perhaps be the means of winning him to the Lord.

"The singing lesson must have been pleasant," she remarked as he sat down beside her before going to his room. He was glad they were alone, for his sister so often tried to tease him, though her mother had told her that her teasing was not helpful to David. Too often it was something that hit him in the place where it hurt the most and she knew that he was unhappy enough without any teasing from others.

He gave his mother one of his rare smiles. "I don't know how successful it was and of course I enjoyed being with her, but she surely gave me a good lecture straight from the shoulder and it made me feel like a heel."

"Good! I'm so glad she did. It's what I've been trying to do for you for years, but without any success."

"But you were always so afraid of hurting me that perhaps that is why your lectures never got across to me." He spoke slowly and with an effort not to stammer — and not succeeding. "She made me take a good look at myself and become aware that I had much to be thankful for, even though I don't have all that I long so much to have."

"I'm so thankful for what she did, son. That's what I've been trying to tell you and what I've been praying about for so long. I'm so thankful for her friendship toward you. I hope that she will continue to be your friend. She will make some man a wonderful wife." She waited hopefully for some response to that remark.

"If any man would ever take the trouble to give her a

second look. Even then, he might not be impressed. He wouldn't realize what a treasure she is."

"Now that you know, how about you, dear? Have you ever thought that you'll need a wife like her?"

He shook his head while his face became serious and a look of sadness crept into his eyes.

"I'll never give a thought of marriage to any girl, no matter how fine or sweet she might be. I've had enough with one experience."

"Don't let one heartless girl ruin your life, David. I'm sure that one day you'll meet some other girl who can make you happy, perhaps a girl as lovely as Janice, but far superior to her in every way."

"But I don't want any other girl," he said stammering, "I still want her, though I'm a fool for still feeling that way."

"You'll get over that in time. I know you will. And in the meantime take Betty's advice and try to make the best of what you have. What did she say about your voice? I'm sure she said that it was good or she wouldn't have wanted to try it out."

He smiled and gave her a look that warmed her heart. He put his arm around her and said tenderly, "I wish I could see myself as you see me. Then I'd have some confidence in myself. She said that I had a good voice and that I should study voice."

"Then why not take her advice?" she reached up and stroked his cheek.

"I'll be too busy to think of anything but my work, if I get the right answer to my application for that job."

"I shall miss you, but I do hope for your sake that you will be accepted. I'm sure that you will give satisfaction and I shall be praying that you will succeed in everything that you undertake. I want you to realize that life is worth living if it is lived in the right way."

Just then his sister Carrie came in and their conversation ended.

Meanwhile Betty was sitting in her room thinking. She couldn't understand why she had fallen in love with David when there seemed to be so little reason for it. Then she rebuked herself for what she had said in her thoughts. It was no twist of fate. Events didn't happen that way in the life of a dedicated Christian and that was what she wanted to be. All that happened to such a one was in the knowledge and the plan of God for that person.

As she sat there, she began to talk to the Lord as if He were visible there beside her. She often did that during her work or during her quiet times, not as a prayer on her knees, but as a talk with friend to friend.

"I don't know why it happened, Lord, but I know that You know and I'm not going to question it. I'm not going to beg You to let David fall in love with me, for if this is in Your plan, I know that it will happen that way, and if it isn't, I know that it will die from my heart. All I want is to be yielded to You. If it is Thy will for him to love me, I shall be so happy, but if this is something that has come into my life to give me more strength even in disappointment, I shall be yielded to Thy will."

There was peace in her heart, even though she knew that she and David would soon be going in different directions and might never meet again.

When she went downstairs and joined her mother, she had a smile on her face and no one would have suspected, even her mother who knew Betty so well, that she had just passed through what to some might have seemed a crisis or severe testing, but which was to her, just another precious experience of her faith and trust in her Lord.

A few days later David received the hoped-for answer to his application. He was elated, for he knew that he would have an opportunity to have a part in some important experiments.

He hastened to tell Betty the good news and she rejoiced with him.

"Let's keep in touch," he suggested. "If you'll write to me, I know what a help it'll be. I'll have a hard time getting adjusted and having to meet all those strangers. They'll likely think I'm a freak, especially when I begin to stutter. I dread that ordeal."

"I'll be glad to keep in touch with you. Write to me and I shall write as long letters as I can, but remember that I shall be burning the midnight oil as well as doing some work in the daytime. I'll always be glad to hear from you."

On his way home David came face to face with Janice. It was the first time he had seen her since that scene he'd never forget.

He nodded and would have passed her, but she stopped him.

"Don't pass me up like that, David, please," she said in her most pleading tone. "I've been wanting to see you again and to apologize for what I did to you, but I never saw you and I was afraid you wouldn't read my letter, if I wrote it."

"I — m — ight not have read it," he said coldly, though, even yet, the sight of her stirred his heart to wild longing. He longed even now to hold her in his arms and feel the touch of his lips against hers. The memory of that attempted kiss lingered with him, even though his anger burned at the memory of what had followed.

"You just don't understand, David," she said in low, tender tone. "I didn't mean to do that to you, because you are so very dear to me, but you just took me by surprise and I acted without thinking."

"Is that always the way you act when you're surprised?" he asked witheringly as he finally got the first word out.

"Now you're being mean to me," she said with that disarming pout. "You just don't understand. You're not the first boy I've had to slap for presuming to kiss me just because I was nice to him. It was different with you, please believe me. You're different from the others. Some of them were playing along with me, but I know you were in earnest. You were, weren't you David?"

"Wh — a — t difference does it make now? Just forget it."

"I can't forget it," she asserted. "It's been worrying me ever since it happened. I want your love, David, for you're very dear to me, as I've told you before, but I'm not ready to fall in love with anyone yet. I want to be free to have many friends, but when I think of those I care for most, you're at the top of the list. Please believe me that you are."

"I — I don't want to be at the top of any girl's list," he stammered. "I want to be the only one or nothing."

"Just give me time and perhaps you will be. Please have patience with me and forgive me for doing what I did without thinking. You're not like those others whom I had to keep in their place. Let's be friends, if you don't any longer want to be something more than friends."

"There won't be any need of either," he stammered. "I'll be going away soon, so just forget me."

"I can't forget you, David. Will you let me write to you?"

"I can't stop you," he said, but the thought of hearing from her thrilled him even though he still smarted under the humiliation of that previous experience.

"May I have your address?" she asked humbly.

"I don't have it with me, but you know the name of the company that I applied to for the job," he told her.

"I shall miss you. Let me wish you the best of everything with your job."

"Thanks," he replied unsmilingly, then they parted.

There was a little smile upon her full, red lips. He still cared for her, in spite of what she had done. Perhaps she would write to him. It was nice to know that he cared, even if she couldn't endure the thought of his kiss. She didn't care at all for him, but it was nice to be admired by so many. Youth and beauty wouldn't last forever and she meant to get the most out of life while she still had both.

As David continued on his way he was sorry he had met her. He had hoped to forget her. He could never be happy unless he could forget her. His new resolution to try to look at life from a different angle grew very weak and the memory of Betty's words of encouragement were in the background of his thoughts. But Janice and her beauty and his love for her still remained.

CHAPTER ELEVEN

DURING THE SHORT TIME that remained before Betty left, David was with her as often as he could manage. She managed an hour or so with him during the few days remaining. The night before she was to leave, he came over for just a few minutes to tell her good-by.

She told him how glad she was that he would be going to work before long and she added that she would be praying daily for him, that he would have every good thing that life could bring.

"I shall miss you terribly," he told her when he rose to leave. "Being with you has helped me more than you can ever know. When I'm with you, I feel I can find the courage to go ahead and be happy, but when I get away from you, I sink back into the depths again. Perhaps if I had known you back in the days when I first began to stutter, you might have helped me over that dreadful time and I never would have developed this terrible affliction."

She laughed. "That was back in the days when we were both too young to know much about what I've been trying to make you believe. I'm afraid I needed help then as much as you did. And then, perhaps you wouldn't have listened to me any better than you do now."

"That was a stupid remark to make, wasn't it? But even then, I know that you would have been my friend when I didn't have a single one. I shall always be thankful for one thing and that is that I have had the privilege of having your friendship now."

"And I'm so happy to have you for my friend — and that I could be a friend to you. I believe that it was all in the plan of God for us to meet when we did and I shall be thankful if you can begin to believe what I've been trying to make you believe."

"I never thought of it that way. I wish I *could* believe some of the things you believe, but I just don't seem to be able to."

"I wish you could," she said as her eyes met his serious ones. "If you could only find the joy that salvation brings and the strength the Lord gives the one who is yielded to Him. It gives such peace to believe God's Word that all things work together for good to those whom He has chosen, to those who are yielded to Him. When you have God, you have everything. When you don't have Him, you really have nothing worth-while. I shall keep on praying that soon you will be willing to let Him take full control of your life, for then I know you will be happy."

As she watched him go, there was a deep yearning in her heart that he would soon find peace and assurance for his life. Though she loved him and would miss him as much or more than he would miss her, there was no rebellion because of her longing for his love. There was only the hope and prayer that he would have the best in life that only God could bestow.

To her surprise, David was at the airport when she arrived and he remained nearby until the last good-bys were said. Since her mother and father were with her, he didn't want to intrude. But she called to him to join them during those last few minutes before she left for New Orleans and a new life.

David stood watching until the plane soared out of sight, then he sighed as he turned away and started toward the taxi stand. He met the Parkers on their way to their car and they insisted that he ride home with them.

During the drive he tried to tell them how much Betty had meant to him and what a help she had been, but he struggled over the words and failed completely. Mrs. Parker kindly helped him out by her understanding remarks.

"Betty enjoyed your friendship. She said that you had such a fine mind and she was eager to encourage you in the work you were soon to undertake. It gave her so much pleasure to know that she was really helping you."

During the next few days after Betty had gone, David experienced loneliness such as he had never felt before. As Betty had told him, he had never sought friends since his experience as a child with his playmates. Consequently he had never had friends. He had never sought Betty's friendship, but she had sought him, because she saw how lonely and withdrawn he was. If she hadn't done that, they would never have been friends and he would have missed what was to be such a blessing to him in the days ahead.

Not long after Betty left, he was busy with his own preparations for a new life in a new world, a world where only success in his work would count.

He was nervous about meeting the head of the department where he was to work, but he found Mr. Simpson a very kind and understanding person. Soon he was at ease as he sat and talked with him. At first he was terribly embarrassed and nervous and because of that nervousness he stuttered more than usual.

"I — I — m sorry," he managed to say after the first attempts to talk and answer questions. "I should have told you what a handicap I have. Perhaps you won't want me to work here." His tone was apologetic and the distressed expression upon his face and in his eyes, touched the man's heart. Ward Simpson was an understanding person and he was also a Christian.

"Don't let your speech impediment get you down," he advised. "What we're interested in is your ability to deliver the work that we require from you and your replies in the questionnaire we sent you make us feel that you can do the work we shall expect. It is your ambition to succeed and your willingness to give of your best that will count, not the way you speak," he added with a smile.

His words, the kindliness in his eyes and his voice put David at his ease and he was able to talk with more freedom.

"Thank you, sir," he said, speaking slowly and trying to avoid the stammer. "I appreciate that. I shall do my best to give satisfaction."

"Good! Then perhaps you'd like to meet the others in your section. I'll introduce them to you," and he rose and led the way to the part of the plant where David was to work.

When they entered the large enclosure and David saw the men there ready to begin the day's activities, he felt absolute panic at the thought of having to get acquainted with them and having to talk to them. He wished he had never come.

Mr. Simpson's remarks after he had introduced the men to David, surprised him, then embarrassed him and finally greatly relieved his nervousness.

"Boys, I shall expect you to remember one thing about your new associate and to act accordingly. David has a speech impediment, but that doesn't mean that he has less ability than any of you and I want you to remember that and to respect this handicap and treat him as one of you. He has ability and I'm sure he will be a great help in the work we're undertaking. So don't underestimate him and above all, don't any of you dare to make him uncomfortable because he may not be able to talk as fast as some of the rest of you, some who may have too much of a gift of gab," and he smiled.

The others returned that smile and some of them assured Simpson that they understood.

Mr. Simpson showed David where he would be situated, then as they left, he asked David where he was staying. David told him that he was at the hotel some distance from the plant. Mr. Simpson told him that he would meet him that afternoon after work and take him to a good boarding house not far from the plant.

When they had left, one of the men in the place turned to the others and asked, "What do you think of our new playmate?"

"He's no beauty, I'll admit," one of the others replied, "but as the big boss reminds us so often, we mustn't judge a person by how he looks, but how he can deliver."

"Yep, that's true," agreed one of the others. "We'll have to wait and see how he delivers. We surely won't be bored by too much chatter from him."

The others laughed, then one of them said, "Just remember the warning. If he's not happy here with us, we'll get a reprimand. There's steel beneath those kind words of the boss."

"You're right, but it's the steel behind those gentle words that keeps everything going smoothly here and it keeps us from the trouble that other plants have been having. He's what I would call a real Christian gentleman."

"I agree with that," one of the others said and the rest agreed with him.

Though they might not know the real meaning of Christianity, they recognized something in Simpson which commanded their respect and their loyalty.

CHAPTER TWELVE

When David reached his hotel, he sat down and looked out the window, trying to regain his composure. He had not realized what an ordeal he would face when he met so many strangers. It was far worse than he had expected.

He had determined not to be nervous and he tried to remember Betty's words of encouragement. But when he had seen all those pairs of eyes looking him over, his courage had failed. He had no idea that there would be so many in his department. So much depended upon a first impression and he felt he had failed miserably to make a good impression.

Though he appreciated Mr. Simpson's words of introduction and especially his words of warning, he hoped that they would not react against him.

He was overwhelmingly lonely, for this was his first time away from his mother and her love. Now there was no one, not even Betty. More than ever, he realized how he had come to depend upon her for her effort to encourage him, even though he hadn't responded to that effort.

He was saddened by the thought that they might never meet again. Some day someone would come along who would recognize her for the jewel she was, as he had said to his mother, and she would marry and be happy. And that one who loved her would always be happy in her love, for Betty had the faculty of spreading her sweetness and cheerfulness to those about her.

How often she had lifted him out of his gloom, if only for a little while, even though he couldn't accept her belief and assurance that through faith in God, he might possess the same peace and cheerfulness she possessed.

Though he longed to possess what she had, there was no desire to meet the condition attached to it. After he had been

with her and had listened to her as she spoke of her faith in
God and the joy in her life because of that faith, he felt impelled
to seek that faith for himself, but he found it didn't come by the
mere determination to possess it. And he had not yet been willing to ask God for it. His old bitterness and despondency
gradually returned to bring on the old unhappiness and hopelessness.

The hours dragged slowly as David sat thinking of the past
and wondering what the future would be. When it was time
to eat, he went down to the dining room because he didn't
know where else to go. He knew that the meal would be expensive and he had to be careful with the money that had been
given him until he could get his first pay check.

The memory of the way that money had come to him
brought a new wave of hurt. His father had turned over the
amount to his mother and she had given it to him, telling him
that his father wanted him to have all that he needed until
he could be on his own. She emphasized his father's concern for
his welfare, but it didn't deceive David.

"Then why didn't he give it to me himself?" David asked.
"He never even said he was proud of me when I made the
valedictory, or that I had been accepted in this good position,
as you did."

"Your father has many worries right now, David, worries
about the business that hasn't been going so well. If things
don't improve, he may lose his job. Try to understand."

David shook his head. "I have tried, all my life, to understand why he has treated me as he has all of these years. I
know now. He just doesn't care anything for me. He never has
cared. I suppose he's glad to get rid of me so he won't be
ashamed of me when we're around others and he has to make
excuses for me."

"David! Don't say that!" his mother cried.

"Why not?" David asked. "I've known it ever since I was
old enough to understand. When I was little, I was afraid of him
because of his coldness and the way I caught him sometimes
looking at me. Then later on when I was older, I heard the two
of you talking about me. It was after he had made you cry for
the way you had treated me. I learned the truth then and it hit
me right between the eyes. I've never forgotten it and I've
never forgiven him for it. It's because I wasn't good looking like

Sis and I don't have the gift of gab that she has. I'm like that creature in some of those fairy tales that you used to read to me. I'm a changeling."

He saw the tears in his mother's eyes, but that didn't stop him.

"In that fairy story the changeling turned out to be a prince and a very handsome young man, but I just stayed the same way I was born and I suppose I'll stay this way until I die."

"Oh David!" she cried through her tears. "I love you, no matter what you say about yourself. You're beautiful to me, because I know that there could be something within you that will one day make you beautiful within. Please don't let your looks make your life filled with bitterness. I know that some day you will hear your father say that he is proud of you. Please believe that, for I pray for it every day."

"That would really take a miracle and you know that I don't believe in miracles."

"But I do," she maintained," and I'm not going to give up believing that that day will come."

The memory of that talk brought added gloom to him as he remembered those last days at home and the last parting before he left for the airport. His sister had kissed him and wished him every success and happiness and he knew that she meant what she said, for though they had never been close, he knew that it had been his fault. Because of their mother, his sister had a genuine affection for him. His father had given him a handshake and had said, "Good-by. I hope you make good on the job. If you need anything, let us know."

If he needed anything! He had never needed anything from him except the one thing that had been denied him, love.

When it was time for Mr. Simpson to pick him up, David went down and waited for him. He came presently and they left for the boarding house.

There he introduced David to the landlady, a pleasant looking elderly woman who tried to make him feel welcome.

"Our boarders are more like a big family," she remarked. "Most of them work at the plant. I know you'll find them congenial, for Mr. Simpson never sends anyone here who might not be. In fact I don't believe he'd even accept any other kind to work under him."

David tried to express his appreciation and, as usual, stammered in embarrassment, while she looked sympathetically at him. He wished that people wouldn't always have that sympathetic look or that look of surprise as he floundered over his first word. If they'd just go on and pretend there was nothing unusual about him, he could stand it better.

His room was comfortable, but it was different from his room at home, with all of his treasures that cluttered it up. Loneliness assailed him as he stood looking around after the others had left. He almost wished that he was back at home and had tried to get some position there. He would at least have been in familiar surroundings with his mother and with people who knew him and wouldn't make him so miserable when he tried to talk to them.

The memory of Janice and of his father made him realize that it was best for him to be where he was. He'd do everything in his power to succeed here where he was. Perhaps the dream he'd had when he was a little fellow, would come true. Perhaps his father would realize that there was something worth-while within him in spite of the way he looked and talked.

With this hope and the determination to make the most of what he had, he finally went to bed and to sleep.

The next morning he faced the ordeal of that first day on the job and it was with increasing nervousness that he reached the plant and sought his appointed place.

The others already there greeted him cordially and gradually his nervousness lessened. They were quite friendly as they gave him a few instructions about his work and the routine for the day and he became more cheerful than he thought he would be. If they noticed his stammering, they gave no hint that he was any different from the others and by the time the noon bell rang, he was pleased with himself, that he had been able to do good work and to fit into the routine without any difficulty.

Several of the others told him what a good start he had made and he began to feel more cheerful and to hope that he could be successful in the work that lay ahead of him.

As for his outlook on the future where other problems were concerned, he felt that at least during the daylight hours there would be little time to ponder over them. It would be better to let them be and to let the future take care of them. He would live in the present and not worry about the future.

He remembered Betty's words that the future for everyone was in the hand of God and that eternity was in the hand of man, whether he would spend it in eternal joy or everlasting grief and suffering beyond the mind of man to conceive. *Was that true?* he wondered.

CHAPTER THIRTEEN

MR. SIMPSON took a special interest in David, for he realized how self-conscious he was and how embarrassed because of his handicap. He knew that David would be lonesome in a strange city and in new surroundings.

Since he was a dedicated Christian, he was interested in the spiritual condition of those with whom he came in contact in his work. The men in his department joked about his attempt to witness to them when the opportunity came. They called it preaching when he sometimes reminded one of them that there was something else in life besides the ambition to succeed in business and make money.

He never forced his views upon them, for he knew that it would only irritate them, but there were frequent occasions when he felt that the right words said at just the right time might make someone think about his need for the love and protection of God in his life.

Though the men joked about him and his "preaching," they respected him and did their utmost to do their best in their work. There was no idling and killing time, for they knew that though he was kind and considerate, he expected the best from them and would not tolerate anything less.

His kindness and interest in them and their welfare was demonstrated when one of them was seriously hurt in an auto accident. The man had a wife and a family and when Mr. Simpson went to visit him in the hospital he saw how worried the young fellow was because they were in such dire need. Though he had insurance to cover his hospitalization for a limited time, there was not enough to cover the cost of the operation and to take care of the length of time he would be absent from work.

Mr. Simpson not only helped the family while the man was recuperating, but his kindness and his "preaching" demonstrated that he lived what he "preached." As a result, both the injured man and his wife were won to the Lord.

When he returned to work, the others observed that he was different. There was a change in him that puzzled them for a while. Though he joked with them about many little incidents that came up during the day or some news item that they commented on, he never smiled or seemed to appreciate a joke that bordered on uncleanness. Finally one of the others asked him what had changed him.

"What's happened to you, fella? Have you gone and got religion?" he asked jokingly.

"Yes, you guessed it," the man replied. "It happened because of Mr. Simpson. When I was down and out and didn't know how I was going to pay all those hospital bills and take care of my family, he not only loaned me the money to pay my bills, but he gave me enough to tide me over and take care of my family until I could get back to work. Because he was so kind, I really listened to him when he talked to me about accepting Christ as my Saviour. I knew that what he had done for me wasn't just because he felt sorry for me, but because he wanted me to see what the love of God could do for a person. He lived it and so I wanted it and I found it. I'm glad that you see that I'm different, because I know I am, thanks to him."

His words made the others think more seriously about what Mr. Simpson had been trying to tell them. They no longer joked about his preaching, but listened with more interest and respect. It was perhaps because of this that they were more sympathetic with David than they might have been otherwise.

When the end of the week came, David faced a lonely week-end. He wondered what he should do to help him pass the time. He was homesick, but hated to admit it. He missed his mother, but he also remembered with a twinge of conscience how he had often refused her when she had asked him to go to church with her. He had been so rebellious when as a youngster he'd had to go, but now he looked back on that time and he was sorry for having hurt her. When he grew older, she no longer tried to force him to go, for she knew that she had tried to influence him in the right direction when he was in the impressionable age and that, now when he was older, it would do no good to make him go against his will. He was old enough to make his own decisions.

For once in his life, his father had been on his side. Since he himself never attended church, he didn't see any reason why David should be urged to go when he didn't want to. So neither of them went and a sad mother and wife and young daughter went together.

As David was preparing to leave the plant, Mr. Simpson came in and spoke to him.

"I was wondering what you plan to do on the week-end."

"I don't have any plans," David admitted.

"I wonder if you care for music," Mr. Simpson asked.

"Yes, I do," David replied.

"Then perhaps you'd like to go to a concert tomorrow night. Ted Harrington is to be here. Perhaps you've heard of him. He's one of the rising young concert singers and this is his first appearance here. I have tickets for three. My wife and I are going, but my daughter has another engagement, so if you'd like to go with us, we'd be glad to have you."

"Oh that would be wonderful!" David stammered. "I'd love to go."

"Then I'll pick you up," and he named the hour. David thanked him and they parted, while David went to his boarding house happy at the prospect of spending a pleasant evening and not having to sit alone and wishing he was at home.

As he sat in the audience, listening to the young tenor's voice, he envied the singer's handsome face and his engaging personality. If he only had just a little of what that singer had, he would be willing to take Betty's advice and try to make something worth-while of his voice. What a joy it would be to sing before an audience who would enjoy his singing as they were doing now, listening to that other singer.

He asked the same question over again. Why was it that some had everything and he had so little? Why! Oh why! Again bitterness cut deep within him. What was the use of wishing for something that could never be?

For a while he was lost in his disconsolate thoughts and failed to listen to the singer. If he could still have been near Betty, perhaps he might have had the courage to be something more than the clod he felt himself to be, but she was not near and she likely never would be. Their paths were far apart and there remained only a memory that would likely grow dim as time passed.

It didn't occur to him that if he had only consented to accept what Betty had, he might be as beautiful within as she was and that same beauty would show through and make others see in him what he saw in her.

He was recalled to the present by loud applause as the young singer returned to take another bow and the audience continued to applaud.

As they left the auditorium and went to the car, Mr. Simpson remarked, "That young man has a great future ahead of him."

His wife agreed and David managed to say a word of agreement also.

Mrs. Simpson was such a friendly person and she was so pretty that David liked her from their first meeting and he didn't feel much embarrassment after his first attempt to talk to her, for she just went on talking as if she hadn't noticed his effort to get out that first word.

When they reached his boarding house, Mr. Simpson turned to him.

"How about going to church with us tomorrow and having dinner with us afterwards?" he asked.

David was pleased at the invitation, but he was aghast at the prospect of having to sit at the table with this strange family.

As David hesitated, Mr. Simpson thought he knew the reason and he hastened to put David at ease.

"There will be just my wife and myself. My son and daughter won't be there. We'd love to have you. I know you'll enjoy the music of our church choir and you won't go to sleep when Pastor Martin preaches."

"We'd love to have you, David," Mrs. Simpson assured him.

David thanked them and said he would be glad to come, though he felt it wasn't quite the truth. He'd rather sit in his room over the week-end than have to attend church and perhaps meet a number of strangers. But he knew he couldn't refuse such a kind invitation, for he realized the thoughtfulness that had prompted it.

There was a smile upon his lips as he told them good-by, but there was no smile in his heart. There was panic at the thought of going to that church and having to meet more strangers.

CHAPTER FOURTEEN

DAVID DREADED THE ORDEAL of going to church more and more as the time drew near for the Simpsons to pick him up.

When they came and he was in the car Mrs. Simpson talked to him, trying to make him feel at ease with them. She realized that he was not quite at ease in her presence, for he revealed it plainly.

She began to ask him questions about his home and family and she related little incidents in her home and with her children who were near his age. Gradually he began to feel more at ease. By the time they reached the church, he had almost forgotten what lay ahead of him.

When they met friends outside the church as they went in and they introduced David, he had only to nod and smile as he acknowledged the introduction, for Mrs. Simpson did the necessary talking.

When they rose to sing the opening hymn, Mr. Simpson held his book so that David might look on it with him. He was afraid to start singing at first, but as they continued and Mr. Simpson's voice rang out loud and unrestrained, he joined in, singing timidly at first, but as the song progressed, he also let his voice out and sang with enjoyment to the close.

When the preacher began to speak, David listened apathetically and the sermon didn't stir his interest as Mr. Simpson hoped that it would, for it was such an appealing message of salvation, emphasizing the love of God and His yearning over every lost soul.

On their way home, Mr. Simpson remarked, "Did you know that your voice has possibilities? But of course you must know. Have you ever thought of having it trained?"

"A friend suggested it," David admitted, "but I never dared to bother with it."

"But you may be missing an opportunity to use it, perhaps in some great way."

He didn't mention what that great way might be, for he knew that it wasn't the time nor the place to suggest that his voice might be used for the Lord.

"Think about it," he advised. "It would give you something to do to keep you from being lonesome until you get better acquainted and I'm sure you would really enjoy learning."

David admitted that what Mr. Simpson said was true, but he had no desire to do what was suggested.

"I'm sure the choir would be glad to have you join them," Mrs. Simpson remarked. "They are always looking for good male voices. Perhaps you'd let me introduce you to the choir director."

"Oh no!" David cried. "I c — ouldn't do that. I just couldn't!"

They understood and they were both sympathetic.

"Perhaps later on when you have had a chance to meet a few of the choir members, you might change your mind," Mrs. Simpson offered.

He was silent, for he knew he never would. He could never face that congregation, even if he stood in the back row.

They invited him to go with them to the evening service, but he begged off and they didn't insist, so after the meal was over, which he enjoyed in spite of his trepidation, he was left alone for the rest of the day.

He wrote to his mother, for he knew that she would be anxious to know how he was getting along. Though he felt ashamed that he hadn't written before, he had felt so depressed he didn't have the heart to write.

He missed her more as the days passed. Now there was nothing in his life but emptiness and an ache, in place of the love that she had bestowed upon him.

Though he had promised to write to Betty, he had no desire to write. There was nothing of real interest to write about. He thought that they would not likely meet again and though he missed her terribly, he felt that there would be little value for either of them in letters. It was her presence that he longed for, not her letters.

He tried not to think of Janice, but thinking of her had become such a habit for so long that it was not easily broken.

He wished even yet, that there could be a fairy tale ending to that chapter in his life, that some day he would return home a person of honor or importance and that she would see him and come to him and ask for forgiveness. He would enjoy freezing her with a look and seeing how surprised and crushed she was.

He sighed as he realized how foolish and childish his dream was. There were no fairy tale endings in lives these days and if there were, he knew that there was no possibility of such an ending coming to him.

It was in this mood that he finally dropped off to sleep. While he was sleeping, in far-off New Orleans Betty was poring over her lesson for the next day, trying to keep her eyes open as she fought sleep. She had been so busy at the hospital all day that she had not even been allowed to go to church, nor did she have time for study.

She was wondering if she had made the right choice in selecting this hospital for training. It had the reputation of being one of the best institutions where experience could be had in treating tropical diseases. She was interested in this, because she knew that she might yet go to the mission field and if she felt called to that work, it would likely be somewhere where she would need such experience.

She soon realized, however, that she would have little or no opportunity to do any real work in trying to win souls. Though this hospital was a state institution, there were rules that no nurse was allowed to teach or talk about "religion" to the patients. This hampered her and she chafed under the prospect of seeing a patient dying or near death and not being able to point that one to eternal life.

She knew that if she should change or ask for a transfer to some other hospital, she would lose credits and she wanted to become a registered nurse as soon as possible. When that became a reality, she could then be free to do what was the most important object of her life, to witness and try to win souls for the Lord.

As she finally closed her book and began to get ready for bed, she thought of David and wondered how he was getting along. Why hadn't he written and given her his address, she wondered. She still hoped that she could have an influence upon him that would finally bring him to seek God's forgiveness. She was honest with herself and admitted that she wanted to hear from him, not only because she hoped to win him for the Lord, but because even a few lines from him letting her know that he still thought of her and needed her help, would make her happy and add cheer to the busy lonely days.

He still cared for Janice, she knew, in spite of his bitter experience. She hoped that he would outgrow that love, not for her sake, but for his, for she knew that the thought of love for her had never entered his mind.

She wished that love had not even entered her mind, much less her heart. David was not a Christian and that even if the impossible should happen and he would fall in love with her, it would only make both of them unhappy.

She still couldn't understand why she had fallen in love with him and she wished that it had not happened, but she decided not to let it worry her or make her unhappy. She had prayed that the Lord would take that love out of her heart or else enable her to overcome it, but her prayer had not been answered, at least not the way she hoped for, so she decided to let it remain in the Lord's hands. She would continue to be happy in Him and endeavor to make her life count for something for Him.

CHAPTER FIFTEEN

TIME PASSED UNEVENTFULLY as David became accustomed
to the routine of his work. It was interesting, for his department had a vital part in some of the company's experiments and
he was as eager as the others were to contribute to the success
of what was being attempted.

Mr. Simpson did everything possible for him to try to make
life pleasant for him without showing any favoritism. David
was so appreciative of his kindness that he often worked over-
time to get certain things finished for which he was responsible,
in order to get that particular project finished ahead of time.

Simpson saw his effort to please and he appreciated what
he saw. He'd had experience with others in David's position at
the plant and their work had been so unsatisfactory that he'd
had to let them go. He was more than ever interested in David's soul and he tried to arouse David's interest by a word or
two now and then, but he saw that his efforts were not pro-
ducing any visible results.

David still went to church with them, for he felt that he
couldn't refuse, but he seemed to have no interest in what he
heard and he refused their further suggestion that he should
join the choir.

When Mrs. Simpson became ill for several weeks and Mr.
Simpson didn't go to church, David wasn't interested enough
to go alone. He drifted on, making no new friends and living
more and more within himself, lonely and unhappy, with but
one desire in life — to succeed in his work and to try to make
the best of what came his way.

As Christmas drew near and he knew that the plant would
be closed during the holidays, he wondered what he should do.
He wanted to see his mother, but there was no joy in the prospect
of going home when he thought of his father and his indif-

ference. It would be better to stay away than to be hurt by his father's coldness.

While he was debating this, he received a letter from his mother that brought tears. It was such a tender plea for him to come home for the holidays that he felt he couldn't refuse. His father had been quite ill, she said, and that was the reason she hadn't written sooner. She told him that for a time he was so low that the doctors gave her no hope, but she had prayed and God had answered her prayer and let him live. When he began to recover, she saw that a change had come over him. He seemed less indifferent to spiritual truths and she was hoping that being so near death he would take stock of his life and give it to the Lord.

She repeated how she had missed him and how she longed for this little time with him. David knew that he should answer her request, so he made his preparations to go home.

His father and mother were both at the airport when he arrived. He was surprised to see his father there. He couldn't help but remember with what bitterness he had left because of the way his father had treated him, but his bitterness vanished when he saw how thin and frail his father looked. The change in his appearance shocked him.

His father was more cordial than he had ever been with him and David was surprised and pleased. Perhaps he might one day be able to compensate to his father for his disappointment in him and somehow he might be able to make him proud, though he had no idea how this could be.

His sister was at a party and wasn't there to meet him, but when she came in she greeted him noisily and breezily and again he was pleased and surprised. He didn't know that some of the greeting from both father and sister had been the result of a lecture that his mother had given them before he arrived. She had told them that if they didn't do everything possible to make David's homecoming happy, she would feel that they didn't care anything for her, for his happiness meant more to her than her own, because he had so little to make him happy.

When Sunday came, David knew that his mother would hope that he would go to church with her and he knew that he couldn't refuse, but he was surprised to see that his father was also going.

He scarcely heard a word the preacher said for he saw

Betty sitting in the choir. Now and then he could get a glimpse of her from where he sat and he was hoping that she would turn and see him, but her eyes were fixed upon the preacher. What had she been doing all these long months? He was ashamed that he hadn't written to her in all this time. He couldn't have told her the truth, that he thought they would perhaps never meet again and that there was no use keeping up a correspondence that could mean nothing to either of them. Maybe he would have the opportunity to see her for a little while during their stay and he hoped even more that she wouldn't be angry with him for not writing.

When the service was over, he waited for her to come out while his family were meeting with friends. When she came out and saw him, there was a pleased, surprised smile upon her lips and a light in her eyes that brought a glad smile to his lips.

"David! What a surprise!" she cried as she held out her hand.

He took both her hands in his and held them while they smiled into each other's eyes.

"How good it is to see you again when I thought I never would," he said as his hands still held hers. "I didn't think you'd be coming home for Christmas and I didn't expect to either."

"I wouldn't have, but I got a special leave of absence because I knew that I might not be able to see my family again for a long time."

"When may I come to see you? I have to see you, if only for a little while before I have to leave."

"I'm surprised that you want to see me at all, for you never wrote and I was so anxious to know how you were getting along."

"I'm sorry about that," he said contritely. "I'll try to explain when I see you. May I phone and find out when you can see me?"

"I'll let you know tonight at church," she told him as she gave him a smile.

He knew why she smiled. He wasn't in the habit of going to church and if he really wanted to see her, he would be there to find out when he could.

The day was far happier than David had thought it would be. In the afternoon several of his sister's girl friends came in and they greeted him so cordially that he was pleased as well as surprised.

Though his father seemed to tire easily and soon went to his room to rest, he seemed more cheerful than David had ever known him to be. He asked David about his work and really seemed interested in what David tried to tell him. He appeared pleased when David told him how kind Mr. Simpson had been and he felt more at ease in his father's presence than he had ever been.

When the time for the evening service came, David's mother was happy as well as surprised when David said he was going with them. She knew why he was so willing to go when she saw Betty in the choir.

Betty told him that she would be glad to see him the next evening and he was there ahead of the time she had mentioned.

"I feel so ashamed for not writing to you," he said as soon as they were seated. "I thought of you many times, but I was so down in the depths that I felt even you couldn't help me and I didn't see any use bothering you with my troubles. I so seldom wrote to my mother and she would scold me for not writing more often."

"If I'd had your address, I might have scolded you for the way you neglected me," she told him.

He laughed. "I needed it. I wished for you so many times when I was down, but I was so low I didn't think that there was much that even you could do."

"I was lonesome and homesick at first," she admitted, "but I was soon so busy that I didn't have time to be lonesome and I was happy, even when I was homesick. I'm sure you know the reason why," she added.

"Sure I do, but I don't want you to start preaching tonight. We don't have time for that."

"I've noticed one thing about you, David. You don't stammer quite as much as you used to. I believe that one day you will outgrow it completely."

"Perhaps," he said slowly and with an effort to keep back that stammering. Now that she had mentioned it, he seemed to be more conscious of it and it suddenly grew worse.

"Tell me how you've been getting along in your work. I know that you've done well, because I know that you have the ability to succeed."

"Thanks for that," he smiled. "Perhaps it was your faith in me that helped me."

He told her all there was to tell about his work and about Mr. Simpson's kindness and she told him about her studies and her hope to be placed in some other hospital or else do private duty where she might be able to minister to souls as well as bodies. Then it was time for him to leave.

He didn't realize until he held her hands for a moment and tried to tell her how glad he was to have had this little chance to be with her again, how dear she was to him, for he had never had another close friend and she had been the dearest he had ever had.

He tried to put it into words, but he failed miserably. She understood and it made her heart ache with the love she had for him and the longing to have him know the love of God and the peace and joy that love could bring.

"Though we may not see each other for a long time and perhaps never," she said. "I shall never cease to pray for you, that you may have the very best that life can hold for you and that one day you may see and believe what that best is."

Her voice was low and tender and he was touched as never before by the sweetness and the melody of her voice. As she looked up at him, her eyes glowing with a soft light, she seemed almost beautiful to him and impulsively he bent and kissed her on her forehead and murmured, "Thank you, dearest friend. I shall always believe that and it will help in any dark days ahead that I may have to live through."

It was well for him that he didn't know about those dark days ahead. . . .

CHAPTER SIXTEEN

WHEN IT WAS TIME for David to leave, he was in a much better spirit than when he had arrived. Memory of Betty and her words of encouragement lingered with him and he determined more than ever before to find a brighter outlook on life and to be more cheerful. It would be difficult to change his whole way of thinking, for it had been a fixed habit for so long, but he knew that if he didn't have strength and determination to overcome that fixed habit, he would go through life glum and discouraged.

He was ashamed to admit that he had been pretty much of a clod. No wonder his father had never tried to show any interest in him. He tried to excuse himself for having that feeling toward his father by recalling the conversation he had overheard that revealed his father's true feelings toward him.

If he had been different himself perhaps his father might have been different. He had never tried to win his father's affection, for in the beginning he was afraid of him and later, he didn't care, for he had bitterness and hatred within himself.

He was grateful for the change in his father since his illness, even though there was no love for his father within himself.

When he was ready to leave, his father shook his hand and spoke more cordially than he ever had before as he told David that he hoped he would continue to succeed in his work and make them all proud of him. The words left him with less bitterness in his heart and a hope that perhaps he might one day have some feeling of affection for him.

He was not aware of what had happened between his father and his mother during his father's illness. It was after hope had been given up that he would recover. His wife took this opportunity to say things to which he would never listen before. She told him that he should be thankful to the Lord for giving him another chance to live for Him. Many times she had tried to talk to him about his soul's salvation and he wouldn't listen and she remarked with a little smile, that now she had him where he couldn't help but listen. She reminded him that from now on he would be forced to recognize that he owed his life to God in answer to her fervent prayers.

"Now you're going to start preaching and you know how I feel about that," he complained in a weak voice.

"Yes, if you want to call it preaching," she agreed, "but if I'm persistent, you know that it's only because I love you so much that I don't want you to waste your life and go into eternity where we will be separated forever. I want the best in life for you and you know that the only way to have that best in life is to turn your life over to God. I won't say any more, but I do beg you to think about this and now while you have the time to think about it, please pray that God will forgive you for all the years of bitterness and disobedience of your life."

"You're thinking about David," he murmured weakly.

"Yes I am. I'm grieving over what you have done to him all through his life and how bitterness has warped your life and kept you away from God. Just because he wasn't the son you expected, you let your bitterness toward God be turned against him and you've almost ruined his life. It wasn't his fault that he is what he is and fear of you helped to make him stammer. You remember what the doctor said about that."

"I never did believe what that doctor said. Now you're blaming me for what that boy has become. I think God was punishing me for something that I don't even know about."

"You knew about your bitterness and rebellion because David was what he was and not what you had wanted him to be. I sinned when I married you, knowing you weren't a Christian. Perhaps I was paying for what I had done, though I don't believe He would punish David for what we had done. I know that somehow it's all in the plan of God."

"I'll try to do better," he conceded. "I guess I have been pretty cold to the boy. I'll try to treat him a little better if he comes home for Christmas."

"He may not want to come when he remembers your coldness. Just treating him a little better may be some help, but it won't take the place of the love that you have denied him when he needed it most," she said sadly.

"I couldn't pretend a love that wasn't there," he retorted petulantly.

"If you'd had the love of God in your heart, there would have been love there for him. He needed it more than if he had been just what you wanted in a son. Do try, dear," she urged. "Try to show him that you do care, even if you don't really love him."

"I'll try," he agreed.

She was satisfied with that concession, for she still had faith to believe that her prayers would one day be answered. She would pray that she might have the patience to wait on God according to His word.

As they drove to the airport, she observed that David seemed more cheerful than he had been when he went away the first time. She hoped that it was partly because his father had showed a different attitude toward him.

"We shall miss you more than ever," she remarked. "Having you with us seemed like old times, but I believe the change has been good for you. You seem so much more self-reliant. Your father and I are proud of you."

"I'm glad if you are, Mom, but I don't know about Dad."

"I'm sure he is, David. Your father is not a demonstrative person, but I saw how he felt when he told you good-by. Don't judge him too harshly."

When they arrived at the airport and stepped out of the car, she put her arms around him and kissed him while tears filled her eyes.

"I shall be praying for you every day. I'll miss you terribly," she whispered as she clung to him. "Give of your best and the best will come back to you. Try to trust the Lord who loves you even more than I do."

"I'll try, Mother," he replied as he kissed her and then went into the terminal without looking back, because he was afraid that she would see the moisture in his own eyes.

His mother watched him until he disappeared inside, then she drove slowly away.

David didn't have much time to wait before his plane was called and he walked down the long concourse toward his gate. There were many coming in the opposite direction with those they had met on an incoming plane and David looked them over idly as he walked toward his plane.

Suddenly his heart gave a leap and he caught his breath in a surprised gasp, for coming toward him was Janice hanging on the arm of some boy he had never seen before. Her eyes were looking into the other's smiling face as they walked along in no great hurry. Her face was aglow, as he had seen it many times before when she was with other men and he wondered what little game she was playing with this fellow.

When she saw him she stopped suddenly and waved to him. "Oh, hello, David!" she called while she gave him a smile. "Why didn't you let me know you were coming home for Christmas?"

He gave her a little wave as he passed on without replying.

He knew that what she said was for the benefit of that other fellow. How long would he last, he wondered. Until she found someone more important or some newer victim for her charms.

All the old pain and all the love he had thought dead forever, returned with added strength. Why did he still care for her, when she was what she was? he asked himself. Just what was it that kept him still captive to this love? It was as if some power beyond himself was holding him in bondage to a love that never should have developed in the first place.

He knew that as long as this unwanted love remained within him, he would never have the desire even to think of falling in love with anyone else. His lip twisted in a crooked smile. Perhaps it was just as well if he never did. Who would ever even consider falling in love with him?

As his plane sped through the cloudless sky, he began to think of what happened while he was at home, then his thoughts turned to Betty. His heart warmed at the memory of her and the gloom lifted a little. What a joy her friendship was and how foolish he had been not to have written to her. Her letters might have been just as comforting as her presence had been. He wished that he could have been with her more often during that brief visit. Now perhaps it would be years or never, before they would meet again.

He felt desolate at the thought. Loneliness assailed him and his brief cheerfulness vanished. Life would still be dull and without much hope of improvement.

CHAPTER SEVENTEEN

DAVID GRADUALLY ADAPTED so well to the routine of his work that in time he lost some of his gloom and silence. He made a few friends and was less lonely, for those who worked with him found that he could appreciate a joke and that he occasionally tried to tell one, though he might be a long time in getting it across. He even learned to laugh at his own efforts when he realized how sympathetic and understanding the others were. Gradually he grew more cheerful.

He did his work so well that Mr. Simpson recognized possibilities in him that many of the others didn't possess. Before another year had passed, he was promoted and transferred to another department. This brought both joy and regret to him. He was glad to get the promotion, but he hated to leave the friends who understood and overlooked his handicap. Now he would have to get acquainted with a new group and the old self-consciousness returned and with it, his increased stammering.

For a time he wondered if he had done the right thing in accepting this new opportunity, but as he became interested in his new work, he realized how foolish he had been even to think of refusing when his success in business was all that he had to keep him going. Otherwise he would have nothing.

His last glimpse of Janice had made him realize that. There could never be the happiness that he had so foolishly hoped for in the past.

He went on with his work with even greater determination to succeed and to be content, even if he could never be happy.

He read occasionally of those who had taken their own lives because of despondency and sometimes when he was down in the depths, he thought he could understand why they did such a thing. He knew that he would never have the courage to take his life, even if he had no desire to go on, for though he had never yielded his life to God and there seemed to be no desire within him to do so, he knew that there was a God and he knew that he didn't dare face Him as a self-inflicted murderer. He tried not to think of eternity. When he did, he told himself that perhaps some day he would feel differently about asking God for salvation. Sometimes after he had talked with Betty, he wondered why it was that there was no desire within him to accept Christ as his Saviour, but wondering about it made him uneasy and so he tried to forget and the small whisper of the voice within him was silenced.

He attended church fairly regularly, for he knew Mr. Simpson expected that. He often invited David to go with him and occasionally he was invited to dinner with the Simpsons. Life seemed to go on somehow and he accepted it as it was with what fortitude he possessed, realizing that it could never be much different.

As he accepted this attitude, he found that he was more content than he had ever been and be began to hope that, after all, life might have a little brighter side.

Occasionally he heard from Betty and her letters helped him in this new resolution and attitude. Her letters were filled with little incidents that happened during her daily routine and she always added the fact that she was praying for him, that he would be happy and find the best in life.

He had little news of interest to tell her, but he wrote because he knew that he would soon have an answer. When he received his promotion, he felt that he really had some good news to write and he was happy to receive her letter telling him how she rejoiced in his success.

After she had received her nurse's certificate of registration she wrote to David telling that she planned to leave for some special work, but she didn't say what that work was, or where it would be. She promised to give him her address as soon as she was established, but when the letter came he mislaid it and it went out with the papers in his waste basket.

After he had searched for it, he thought that he would write home and have his mother try to get the address from Betty's mother, for he wanted to continue hearing from her. But that time never came, for before he had time even to write to his mother, he was too upset to even think of Betty.

He received his draft notice. The notice came for him to report for induction at a given date. It came as such a shock that he sat stunned for long minutes, just staring at the wall. He felt that the earth had suddenly dropped from under him, leaving him suspended in space.

That he was subject to the draft he realized, but as yet the war hadn't reached such proportions that inductees were called in large numbers. He hadn't read the papers saying that the President was increasing the draft call, or he might have been better prepared.

When he broke the news of his call to Mr. Simpson, he appreciated the man's regret over losing him, but it didn't lessen his own despair. He felt that his life was already ended and that what little progress he had made toward trying to make the best of life was being destroyed. It wasn't the physical danger to himself that concerned him, but he was grieving over the fact that just when he was in the process of trying to make his life a success in business and when he was already on the way to that success, this should come. If he lived until his term of service should end, he would have to begin life all over again and he just wouldn't have the courage or desire to do that. It wouldn't be worth the struggle.

When he returned home for the little while before he had to appear before the draft board, he was as blue and despondent as he had ever been and even more so.

He was determined not to let his mother know how he felt, for he didn't want to play the coward before anyone. He determined that he'd go overseas and fight the best he could, though he didn't understand why America had ever become involved in this war. It seemed so useless. If it had been when his country was fighting for their very lives and their liberty he could see the reason for that. But there had never seemed to be a good reason for this war, though he had heard and read the many reasons that were given.

Yes, he told himself, he'd go and fight to the death and he wouldn't care very much when that death came, for, after all, it might prove to be the easiest way out.

His mother couldn't keep back the tears when she knew how soon he would have to leave. She tried in every way, without making him resentful, to make him see how important it was for him to make his surrender to the Lord before he had to go into battle and face death, but her words seemed to fall upon deaf ears. There was just no response within him to her carefully chosen words.

When the time came for him to say good-by, his father said words that he had never expected to hear from him. He had turned from his sister who had hugged and kissed him and told him that they would be praying for him. Then as he turned to his father, his father clasped his hand and put an arm around his shoulder.

"Son, I know that you will make us proud of you and when your time is up, we'll be waiting for you with a warm welcome and flags flying."

He added those last words with a smile that David had never seen upon his face before, at least not when he was talking to him.

Tears filled his eyes and he replied in slow, halting voice, "I shall try to make you proud of me."

His mother clung to him and her sobs made her voice weak and shaky as she tried to speak.

"You know that my prayers shall follow you every hour that you're away. I believe God will return you to us. I know that when you return, we'll be proud of you. Don't fail to help God answer my prayers," she added in a whisper as she kissed him and then let him go.

As the plane took him away from all he loved, all that had made life worth living, her love and her own dear self, he wondered at her last whispered words. How could he help God make them proud of him? How could anyone help God? God did according to His will in the affairs of men, so how could he either help or hinder God from doing anything? Hadn't He made him as he was? Hadn't He taken him from the only thing that was giving him hope of making something of his life? Wasn't He leading him into a war from which, if he came out alive, he might be so wounded and crippled that life would be even worse than it had been?

What could any human do to help God, or hinder Him? What was the use of trying to do the impossible?

He should have known, for he had heard it often enough, that the only way a human being could help God was to be so yielded to Him that God could use him not only to help himself and to be happy and have peace within, but that he could be used to be a help to others, so that they might find what he himself possessed. He had heard, but he hadn't heeded.

He gradually became calm as the plane sped on, and he thought of Betty. He could never tell her where he was and he would eventually go to Viet Nam and perhaps die there. That possibility filled him with fear.

He shook himself mentally. Why let his mind linger on such thoughts? He was soon to be in the army and he would do his best to kill as many of the enemy as he could, before they got him.

As the plane flew on through the night he finally fell asleep.

CHAPTER EIGHTEEN

DAVID DIDN'T EVEN WANT TO THINK of the future if he should survive when so many others of his age had already been sacrificed in a war in which he could find no reason nor hope, for he felt that he wouldn't survive.

It still seemed more like a bad dream than reality when he was finally inducted into the service and was off for training before going over to join the conflict which was growing more terrible and extended as the days passed.

He had felt his usual embarrassment when he answered the few oral questions that were asked before he filled out the questionnaire that was given him. The officer who took his application didn't seem to notice his stammering. Perhaps it was because other young fellows who were being torn away from home and loved ones, stammered just because of the upset and the end to all their plans for their lives.

When he saw some of the men in his group, he didn't wonder that they revealed how they felt, for he felt the same way. He knew that it wasn't cowardice that caused the expression upon their faces, or the look in their eyes.

But youth and the ability of most human beings to rise above sorrow and disappointment and to continue to get the most out of life as it came, made them seek their periods of relaxation, when they could gather and try to forget what was behind them and what might be ahead for them.

After hours of training in mucky swamp land, looking for hidden weapons, hidden explosives, or enemy infiltrators, they were allowed their time for rest and relaxation. It was then that they tried to sing popular songs, or play cards in order to forget when memories of home brought heartache.

At first David sank back into his habit of keeping to himself, dreading the laughter or thoughtless jokes about his stammering, but as the days passed and he became more accustomed to his surroundings and better acquainted with his buddies, he was so lonely that he was glad of the proffered friendship of those billeted with him.

It wasn't easy to keep clean when they were constantly creeping through mud and dirt, but he managed to make the best of this new situation together with the rest of them.

"Oh! for a soft mattress and a good clean bed!" sighed one of the fellows as they stretched out upon the grass in front of their billet.

"And a good hot biscuit and some scrambled eggs and bacon," sighed another.

"Longing for what you can't have won't make it any easier to get ready for what's ahead of you," a third one remarked. "Let's forget what's behind us and what's ahead of us and pretend that we're just out here on a picnic and that we'll soon be home again to bacon and scrambled eggs and biscuits. Let's sing something that might cheer us up a bit and help us to forget what we can't help."

One of them started a song that most of them were familiar with and the others joined in, singing in muted tones. David sat silent for a while, feeling too depressed even to try to sing, but as they continued, he finally joined in and forgot for the moment that he was singing louder than the others.

Suddenly he stopped, for he realized that he was singing alone while they were listening in surprise. He stopped in the middle of a word and stared at them with his mouth still open on that last high note. Then he felt his face redden while hurt and anger rose within him. They were laughing at him. He stared at them angrily, anger at himself for trying to sing, and at them for making him look ridiculous.

His anger turned to surprise as they began to applaud him. He thought it was just another evidence of what they thought of him. He was just a clown and he had made himself that in fact while he was only trying to be one of them.

"That was great, fella," said the soldier sitting nearest him.

"It sure was, boy," chimed in another. "Give us that other verse. We want to hear more."

"Stop it!" he cried. "You've gone far enough!"

"Whad do you mean?" cried one of the others. "We're not joking. We mean it. Boy, you've got something that you should be proud of. You've really got a voice. If we ever get out of this mess, you ought to do something with it."

The boy next to David saw that he had misunderstood their applause and he turned a serious face to David, who was still angry and doubting their sincerity.

"Dave, we meant that we really did like your singing. That's why we stopped, so that we could hear you. Don't be angry. You know I wouldn't lie to you."

David turned and looked doubtfully at the boy, Tom Fisher. He had seen this young soldier reading his Testament and he knew that it took courage for him to do that. It also made him remember the little Testament his mother had given him with the tearful request that he would read at least a verse or two whenever he found the time. He had told her that he would, for he didn't have the heart to refuse her in a time like that, but he had never opened the Book. When he saw Tom reading his, the small voice of conscience reproached him.

He turned again to the others looking at him with smiles that he had misunderstood.

"I thought you were laughing at me," he confessed, trying not to stammer and not succeeding.

"Be a good sport and sing something for us," one of them suggested.

"I'm sorry, but I don't know anything else but hymns that I learned when I was a child and my mother used to take me to church," he said.

"Then sing one," Tom suggested. "Something like that is just what we need."

"Go ahead. We can take it," another spoke up. "I guess we do need something to take our minds off of this mud and the mire and filth we'll soon be in overseas."

David still hesitated, but Tom again spoke. "They need something like that and so do I. Go ahead and do what they ask."

Tom knew that some of these boys came from Christian homes, even though they themselves were not Christians, and he was hoping that some little thing like this might make them think, for none was sure he would come out of this alive.

For a moment David still hesitated, embarrassed at the thought of singing with all those eyes looking at him. Then, on a sudden impulse, acting from some unknown prompting from within, he began to sing the one song that always thrilled him whenever he heard it.

His voice rang out, at first rather uncertainly, but growing stronger as he gained more confidence, in the words and melody of that beautiful song, "I'm overshadowed by His matchless love," and on to the end.

When the song was ended, there was silence. There was moisture in the eyes of some of that silent audience and upon their faces were grave expressions.

David sat there looking them over and wondering what had made him do a thing like that. Presently there came to them the faint sound of someone playing softly "Home, Sweet Home." The men slipped away one by one without a word, leaving David and Tom alone.

"David," Tom said and his voice was husky, "the Lord led you to do something tonight that did more for those boys than a dozen sermons could have done. I'm sure that it will have results that you may never know about, but they will be there just the same. I'm so glad that you were obedient to the leading of the Lord. You should praise Him for letting you do a thing like that."

David turned to him and retorted in a tone that hurt Tom more than if he had struck him, "I wasn't thinking about the Lord! He didn't have anything to do with it. I just sang it because- because- Oh, I don't know why I sang it!" and he turned and left Tom who sat there looking after him.

"I know better, you poor fellow!" Tom murmured to himself as he rose and followed David to their tent. "I believe the Lord has laid His hand on you and you'll never get away from Him until you give yourself to Him. Someone at home surely must be praying for you and I shall be praying with them."

As David lay upon his cot staring with wide eyes into the darkness, he was wondering what had happened to make him sing that song when he knew others that he had learned in his childhood. The song made him think of Betty and the time she had sung it for him. A longing to see her and to hear her words of encouragement overwhelmed him. What a joy it would be to hear her voice and to listen to her sweet little way of hinting to him the thing that was on her heart, the things that she loved to mention to him and which she knew that he didn't want to hear. How glad he would be, if he could just get a glimpse of her for a moment. He was sorry that there was no sign of her when he was at home. Now he was gone and she didn't even know where he was. She didn't know that he would soon be on his way to Viet Nam and the horror of that conflict. She might never know until, if he was killed, she would see his name in the list of casualties from their home-town. He wished that he had her address. Now he couldn't even write to her. There was little possibility that he would ever see her again.

He wondered if she would grieve that he was gone, if he should be killed. He thought she would care a little, for her friendship was real.

What made him sing that song, he wondered again. Of course Tom would say that it was of the Lord, but he knew better. The Lord didn't care anything about him, so why should He use him to sing a song that would have any influence upon anyone? Tom was foolish even to imagine such a thing.

When he finally settled down and went to sleep, his thoughts were again with Betty and there was a longing that was like an ache, for at least a word from her, just a glimpse of her, but there was no hope that that could ever be. Not as long as this war lasted — and it seemed that it would last forever.

CHAPTER NINETEEN

DAVID STRAINED HIS EYES for a last glimpse of the shoreline as they headed toward danger, possible injury or death. There was a strange quiet among his group as they, with others, joined the ones sent as reinforcements to stop the ever-increasing advance of the enemy. This enemy was used to jungle warfare and they cared nothing for the ordinary rules of civilized warfare. It was their determination, regardless of how many of their own soldiers they sacrificed, to drive a foreign enemy from a nation which they were determined to conquer and rule. They cared not what destruction was wrought upon helpless natives who lived in daily increasing terror as more and more were left with homes destroyed and loved ones mangled or dying.

David felt that he would never see his homeland again and he was sure that many of the others felt the same way. That did not encourage conversation. When, however, they landed at last and were billeted until they were called into action, the tension lessened and they were interested, in spite of their homesickness and the uncertainty of the future, in this strange new land and its people.

The natives stared at them stolidly and David wondered if they were afraid of them, were sorry that they had come, or were just indifferent. He didn't realize that they had already suffered so much from this long, drawn-out war that they had little emotion left but dull despair. Though he couldn't decide what their emotions were, he saw so much evidence of dire poverty in the little time it took them to travel to where they were to billeted, that he felt terribly sorry for them. He felt a sense of gratitude for the home he had, the supply of all of his needs, where there had never been a day of terror such as these poor people had known for so long, where he had known every comfort and where the terror of enemy invasion had never existed for him.

His thoughts seemed to find echo in Tom's heart, for he remarked while they were waiting for orders and instructions, "Seeing these poor natives with their expressions of hopelessness, makes me appreciate more than ever the blessings that God has given us in America. How thankful we should be for what we have had in a country which, during our lifetime has never had the fear of invasion from any enemy."

"Why does God allow all this?" David asked. "It seems so unfair. What have they ever done to deserve this?"

"Now you're asking something that a wiser head than mine would have to answer," Tom replied. "But I could ask this, what have they ever done to expect anything from God? They are a heathen nation and since they don't have faith in God, do they have any right to expect anything from Him, protection or blessings?"

"How can they have faith in God if they don't know anything about Him? Why didn't God make Himself known to them so that they could trust Him and have His protection?"

"Now you're asking me to go back into the beginning of time and give you a sermon that might be beyond me," Tom told him with a little laugh. "I can tell you this much. In the first chapter of Romans, it tells us that in the beginning they all knew God, way back before there were so many people and so many nations. They knew God, for He had revealed Himself to them in many ways, but they forsook Him and turned to idols and it says that they worshiped the creatures instead of the Creator. Then God turned them over to their own wickedness and vile ways of living, but He sent His prophets and His messengers that we call missionaries today, to tell them of the one true God. Those who heard and believed were saved from their sins and God blessed them and gave them both His protection and His peace. We find proof of that in the book of Jonah, when God sent him to the city of Nineveh to warn them of their wickedness."

"What became of them?" David asked, interested in spite of himself.

If he had ever heard a sermon upon Jonah, he had long ago forgotten it and he had never heard Bible truth presented in the way Tom was presenting it now.

"They repented and God forgave them and gave them another chance, but years afterwards they drifted back into their same sins and they were destroyed."

"That was way back in Old Testament times," David remarked. "What has that to do with these people? How could they ever know that their condition is caused by the way they have lived? How has God given them a chance to turn from their heathenism?"

"They have missionaries right here in their midst. I know of a young man and his family who have been here for a long time teaching these natives the right way. Perhaps we shall see the little church where they worship in when we get going."

Later, when they were on their way out of town, they passed the little church and Tom pointed it out to David as they passed by.

"They can't say they never had a chance, for the Word of God has been preached here at least," he remarked. "I have a picture of that church at home."

"I still don't understand it all," David admitted.

"Neither do I," Tom admitted, "but God knows what He's doing and all I can do or want to do is to believe Him and His Word and pray for these people and all those others who don't have the joy of knowing and worshiping Him."

It was not long before the new troops were in the midst of the fighting, for the war had become intensified and the North Vietnamese were infiltrating into the outskirts of Saigon, causing death and destruction there.

When Christmas came it was a dull day for David's company. They had been for weeks in water-soaked rice paddies, in swamps and on jungle trails seeking for the enemy, their cleverly concealed tunnels and gun emplacements. They realized that some of these tunnels which they found had been dug in long months of preparation before the war even started.

During the time that David had been away from home, he had received only letters from his mother and a few from his sister. Mail was scarce for they were seldom where they could receive it regularly and it was eagerly seized when it came. In several of his mother's letters, she sent a message from his father. It made him realize that his father had changed his attitude somewhat, but he still felt that there was no real love in his father's heart for him. If there was, it had come too late, for he had no love for him.

David had little time to think of anything when they were actively engaged, for this jungle warfare was far more dangerous than if they were engaged in regular battle. They could never tell when they would stumble upon hidden enemy fire from some unseen tunnel. Hidden by jungle foliage, enemy snipers lay in wait for them. It held none of the excitement and the thrill of open warfare, though the danger was even greater, for when they fought an enemy they could see, they could plan their attack and feel the thrill of a victory won with an open conflict, or plan their retreat.

In their rest periods, there was time for much thinking and little inclination for talking, for they were worn and dirty and they longed for a bath, a clean bed and restful slumber. It was in this short time of rest and relaxation that David thought of home and his past life and of the few who really mattered in his life. He envied those others who had such a large circle of friends, who could talk about them when there was time for conversation, about the escapades they and some of their chums had engaged in when they were safe at home with no thought of war. It was his own fault that he had no friends held over from his childhood, for he had never tried to make any. He could only think of the two who had had such an important part in his life, Janice and Betty.

Thinking of them often during hours when he was too tired even to sleep, he wondered if Janice ever gave him a thought. He remembered his foolish dream of one day returning home as a hero and when his hometown people would be proud of him. How he hoped someday to make Janice sorry that she had treated him so terribly.

If he ever returned home at all, he knew it would be to sink back into the old rut of loneliness. He would never love anyone, for Janice had killed something in him. He hated himself for the knowledge that though she had killed something within him, she had not killed the love he still had for her.

In the midst of these thoughts that only added to his unhappiness, there would come the memory of Betty and in his memory her plain little face would always wear the lovely smile that transformed it and made her almost pretty. How wonderfully she had lifted him out of his gloom so many times. If he could only have a word from her, just to let him know that she was still thinking of him and praying for him. He hoped that she was still praying for him, for though he had never had much faith in those prayers for him, he felt a certain amount of comfort in just knowing that she cared enough for his friendship to want to pray for him.

He surely needed her prayers now, for if he had ever been despondent and down in the depths, it was now. There seemed to be no end to this jungle warfare. Already some of the fellows in his company had been injured and three had been killed. The most discouraging thing about it was the knowledge that it seemed destined to go on forever, with no hope of either victory or defeat for either side. How soon his turn would come, of course he would never know.

He just hoped that when the bullet that bore his name should hit him, he would go quickly and not be allowed to lie in agony or to be slaughtered by some hidden jungle fighter.

CHAPTER TWENTY

THE MEN WHO WERE BILLETED WITH DAVID were shaken by their first experience of the horrors of war when their encounter was over and they went out to get their dead and wounded. Though the enemy had been driven back for the time being, they knew that it was only temporary and that they would return in increasing numbers.

It was nearly dusk when they finally brought in those left in that marshy soil. Two who were seriously wounded lay groaning. Another was dead, terribly mangled by some blast that had torn a great hole in his side.

The wounded were taken to safety, then Tom and David returned to carry the one who had been killed back to where they might care for his body until they knew what to do. As they stood there looking down at the still form, Tom uttered a deep sigh.

"I wonder if he was ready to go," he said in low tones.

David heard and the thought smote him.

"He was a good boy," he said, feeling that he had to say something, yet touched and troubled by that whispered question. "I liked him a lot."

"So did all the fellows," Tom agreed. "He was the one who always brought a laugh when most of us were down in the depths with homesickness. But being a good fellow isn't enough and I wonder if Jack had that something else that I tried to talk to him about. I hope he did, but I just wonder. He listened to me when I tried to talk to him about his soul, but he never would get serious about it, even when I tried to make him see that it was the most serious thing in his life — the question of what he would do with Jesus, receive Him or reject Him. I suppose I'll never know until we stand before the Lord. I hope he will be there."

Just then others joined them and they lifted the shattered body and carried it back to camp. That night there was no attempt to linger and talk before falling in. All were too conscious of the nearness of danger and that death was stalking about, waiting for the next victims.

The seriousness of the wounds of the two who had been taken to the temporary hospital made them realize that if they escaped death, life might have little left for them to anticipate, for one of the boys was blinded and the other had a shattered arm.

Tom's words as they stood over Jack's body still rang in David's ears. He knew that he wasn't "ready to go," but there seemed to be some unseen barrier within him that prevented him from doing anything to change his spiritual condition. There was no desire there, just an apathy that prevented him from wanting to do anything about it.

For a time there was a lull in the fighting in David's section and they waited tensely for further orders. Then suddenly the Vietcong invaded the neutral zone with increased numbers and the fighting was intensified all along the lines. As David's division plunged into the jungle, he went with but one desire. That was to kill as many of the enemy as possible before they should get him. Memory of Jack's mutilated body only increased his desire for vengeance and in the heart of the conflict, he had no time for thought of danger to himself.

Guns seemed to be peppering them from all sides from an enemy skilled in this kind of warfare and he saw others go down not too far away as he and Tom plunged forward, trying to keep up with those who had gone on before them.

Then it came. A blast from some hidden fire struck beside them and two of his buddies went down. Then something struck him in the side, seeming to tear his flesh to bits. He felt the blood soaking his shirt, but he was heedless of the blood and the pain, for he saw Tom go down with a sharp little cry and then lie still.

Regardless of flying bullets and the cries of others who had been wounded, he knelt beside Tom and called to him in broken tones to speak to him. There was no response and he knew that Tom was dead. Forgetting where he was, he knelt beside Tom's body and sobbed like a child for a moment, then he stood up and tried to lift Tom's body to his shoulders, but his pain was too great and he felt a fresh spurt of blood from his wound.

The ground was soft, so he placed Tom's body back upon it for a moment, then he lifted him under his arms and began to drag him back out of the muck to safety.

By the time he had gotten beyond the danger zone, the brief encounter had ended and the weary soldiers were returning to their camp, leaving only a few outpost guards. Then they saw David with Tom's still form and they hastened to help him.

"He's dead! He's dead!" David cried brokenly. "The best guy in the whole division and those devils had to kill him! Why couldn't it have been me! Why couldn't it have been me!"

They stood for a moment looking down at the still form and grieving over the death of their comrade, for all of them had respected Tom for what he believed and for the life he lived before them, though at times some of them had joked with him and had tried to "get a rise" out of him. Tom had accepted their good natured ribbing and had answered them with a response that often brought a laugh, though it always contained some nugget of truth that he wanted them to believe.

While they stood looking down at the still form, they uttered exclamations of surprise for Tom opened his eyes and looked at them for a moment bewildered. Then he saw David and he tried to speak.

David knelt beside him, anxious to catch every word if he should speak.

"I'm going — David," he said slowly, having difficulty in forming the words. "It's- best this- way. Remember- I'm happy- to be- with the-Lord. Oh, David-" and the words came more slowly as he gasped for fast failing breath, "Please- get-ready- to go-God- loves you- and I- love-you-in-His name."

His voice died in a whisper and they knew that he was gone.

"If there's any truth in what he believed, he surely was ready to go," one of the fellows remarked sadly. "He sure did believe. Makes a fellow think."

"Hey! You're wounded!" one of them exclaimed to David. "You'd better go and get yourself attended to."

Reacting from loss of blood, the pain and the grief and nervous strain, David slumped to the ground and lay there for a while, trying to regain his strength. Two of them helped him and he was taken to the emergency station.

As he lay upon the cot after his wound had been attended to, he kept thinking of Tom and of the last words that Tom had spoken. How he longed for just one more talk with Tom. Perhaps if he could have had that one last talk, he might have been willing to do what Tom had so often suggested to him. He knew the way, for he had heard it often enough at home from his mother, but there had been no desire for response.

His mother had often wondered why her prayers and her pleas and her teaching had found no response in David's heart. She had finally just turned him over to the Lord. She recalled God's promise that if one should train a child in the way he should go, when he was old, he would not depart from it.

She had told the Lord humbly and beseechingly, "Lord, I've trusted Your Word and I've done my best by teaching and by precept and pleading but he will not yield his heart to You. If you have to take him through a deeper valley in order to save him, I'll just wait and trust Thee."

And she did, though at times her heart ached over God's delay. She remembered that passage in Isaiah that read, "Therefore will the Lord wait — blessed are all they who wait for Him." But waiting was so hard.

In David's heart just then, his feeling was certainly not that of contrition for his sins, nor the desire to be ready to go. There was a feeling of resentment against God.

Why did God have to take Tom when he was the dearest friend he ever had? *Why couldn't He have taken me? What good am I anyway? It just wasn't fair. It wasn't fair!* he groaned inwardly.

His wound proved to be superficial, though painful. A bullet had torn through the flesh of his side and had grazed a rib, damaging it, but not seriously. He was told that his recovery wouldn't take long.

During his brief stay in the hospital, he wondered at the courage and the patience of the army nurses who had volunteered for duty there. They never seemed to tire or to be cross, even though some of the fellows were unreasonable under pain. To him the nurses seemed to be real angels of mercy.

One of them reminded him of Betty, for she always wore

a smile even though there were deep circles of weariness under her eyes.

"How do you always manage to keep so cheerful when I know you're so tired," David asked, stammering, when she was ready to go off duty.

"What's the use of being grouchy?" she replied. "You fellows have suffered enough without having a sourpuss serving you here."

She gave him a smile. "You'll be getting your discharge in a few days and do you know what you're going to get?"

"Another chance to be a target for some sniper's bullet," he retorted.

"You'll be getting a purple heart and perhaps a bronze star when you get home, or perhaps sooner than that."

"If I don't get a wooden cross to mark my grave," he said. He realized that he had just started on a long road that might lead to nowhere but a grave. He was determined that when he got back into battle, he'd try to take as many with him as he could, if he went out, before that cross would mark his grave.

CHAPTER TWENTY-ONE

DAVID'S RECOVERY was slower than the doctors had anticipated. They noticed his apathy and one of them wondered if he was purposely refusing to try to help them in their effort to hasten his recovery. Finally he spoke to David about it, for he was disappointed in David's slow recovery and he wondered if perhaps it was because of some lack of skill on his part.

"What's the matter with you, boy? Don't you want to get well? You're not even trying."

"It doesn't matter to me whether I get well or not, so why should it bother you?" David retorted with a trace of anger. "The sooner I get out of here, the sooner I'll be back, so what difference does it make?"

"You should be out there covering yourself with glory. Wouldn't you like to go home a hero and get your picture in the paper?" the doctor asked.

The thought of having his picture in his hometown paper brought a short ejaculation from David. Of all things, his picture in the paper!

"I'm not even thinking of going home at all," he said slowly and trying not to stammer. "I don't expect to get home. Please go away and let me alone. I'm doing the best I can and you're doing the best you can, so let's leave it there."

Finally he was well enough to rejoin his outfit. Still remembering Tom, they were in a more serious mood than they had been before his death. Then too, they had seen some rough fighting and several more of their number had been killed or were on their way home in serious condition.

After a time, things quieted down in their section, just a few encounters with snipers and no serious results in the American forces. They knew from past experience that the enemy was preparing for another mass attack and another invasion of Saigon.

David had lost track of time. He didn't remember how long it had been since he had had his first encounter with the Vietcong. One day was pretty much the same as another during this lull, a sortie into the demilitarized zone to hunt out tunnels or enemy gun emplacements, sporadic fighting and shots from hidden snipers.

Though he didn't feel as strong as he had before his injury, he fought whenever there was need for fighting, with dogged determination to make as many of the enemy as possible pay for the death of Tom.

Occasionally he thought of Tom's last words and they disturbed him, but there was no time to mull over them and he was glad, for he was intent upon the main business of his life now, to kill as many of the enemy as possible.

As the tempo in his area increased, he became more careless of his own safety, rushing into hidden gunfire recklessly. More than once he came upon the hidden enemy and he ended that fellow's career.

One evening when they had been on the march for some hours, as the sun was low in the partly clouded sky, renewed fury of firing began from the enemy. A number of those who had been in the lead were seen to go down, but the others pushed on into the enemy stronghold hidden among the jungle growth.

David's small group was cut off from the rest of the command and they were alone and seemingly surrounded by gun fire, but they were unable to discover from where it originated. The young corporal who had been leading them in their cautious search fell and lay still. Knowing that he was dead, they stopped for a paralyzed moment, not sure what they should do, to continue their search which seemed to be hopeless or to withdraw.

David hesitated with the others, when he realized that they were without leadership, then he started forward on the run, calling back to the others, "Follow me! Let's get in there and kill those devils, even if it takes the last one of us to do it!"

He plunged into the undergrowth, not looking back to see whether the others were following. He didn't realize that in that moment something had happened to him. There was no stammering in that command, no stuttering hesitation to get that first word out. His words came out like shots from a gun, loud and clear, with authority that somehow the others respected and obeyed.

As he ran he fired in the direction from which most of the shots seemed to come. The others followed his example and in minutes there was a barrage going into that hidden sniper spot.

They heard short cries of agony from within the hidden area and a gradual silencing of the firing until there was none from the enemy. The men following David approached the spot where the firing had been. David, still in the lead, stopped and waved to the others.

"Here's where they came from," he called to them. "There's a tunnel here."

He had found one of the hidden tunnels they had been searching for, but had been held back by enemy fire.

"Let's go in and clean it out," he called back to them as they came closer, still looking cautiously about for more hidden gun fire, but there was none.

David reached the entrance to the tunnel which had been cleverly concealed and he started to enter. Just then, as he crouched over, his foot touched something hard and then the whole world seemed to rise up and strike him, from the top of his head to the full length of his body as he leaned over to enter the tunnel. He felt the stinging and slashing of something like glass across his face and the hurt of what seemed like knives piercing his clothing and slashing his body.

He gave one agonized cry, then fell back and lay there moaning.

The others, after one horrified moment, came nearer and saw that he was still alive, so two of them lifted him to carry him back out of danger, while the others wondered whether they should try to enter the tunnel or leave.

David saw them standing there hesitating and he stopped moaning for a moment and called out weakly to them, "Go on in! There won't be any more trouble. This was meant to discourage us. Don't let this opportunity pass to destroy that hell hole."

He lost consciousness while they obeyed his command to finish what they had begun and they discovered a large cache of arms and ammunition.

When he regained consciousness, he was lying on a cot in an emergency station. Covered with bandages from head to foot, he looked more like a mummy than a human being still alive. His face had been so cut that it was given only emergency aid, for he would have to be shipped home where he could undergo plastic surgery, if he lived to need it. Only his eyes and a space for his nose and mouth was left open. His body had been cut as if somebody wielding a knife had swung about recklessly and slashed him mercilessly.

The doctors who treated him in emergency wondered what kind of a mechanism could have done so much damage in one explosion without blowing him to pieces. They dug out bits of glass from all over his body.

He tried to move before he realized where he was and what had happened, but the movement caused so much pain that he groaned and lay still. He heard a voice that he recognized. It was the voice of the young nurse who had attended him when he had been there before.

"Don't try to move, please," she said in soothing tones. "You'll be more comfortable if you just lie perfectly still until you have a sedative and it will help your wounds if you don't move."

He could only open his eyes partially, but he could see the edge of the bandage over them. He tried to speak, but his mouth was too stiff because of the bandages and he failed to utter a word, but just looked at the nurse and she saw the question in his eyes.

"You're back again, just like you said you would be. You're a good prophet."

She smiled, trying not to reveal her horror at his condition.

David uttered a groan, for he was beginning to feel pain which a merciful unconsciousness had prevented him from feeling before.

"You did a wonderfully brave thing when you led those men into that ambush and knocked those snipers out," she told him, trying to distract him from his suffering. "Your buddies told us about it when they brought you in."

David tried to answer her smile. She surely deserved some reply to her effort to make him forget his pain, but even that little effort to talk caused pain and he couldn't control the groan that escaped his stiff lips.

"You've been a mighty brave soldier," she continued, trying to keep a cheerful expression, for pity overwhelmed her. She didn't expect this soldier to survive this terrible tragedy. If he did, how terribly disfigured he would be!

"I know all of your family and your friends will be so proud of you that you'll just about burst with pride yourself," she babbled on, hoping that the orderly would soon come with the sedative.

She felt that she couldn't take much more. As she looked at that mummified figure staring at her so hopelessly through those slits of his eyes, she felt close to tears.

Presently the sedative was brought in. As he saw David, the orderly uttered a gasp. "Boy! This is a bad one!" he cried in low tones. "I don't see how you can find a place to put the needle."

"Sh!" the nurse cautioned. "Just give it to me and I'll find a place."

David hadn't heard, for he had again drifted into merciful unconsciousness.

The nurse stood for a moment looking at him while tears filled her eyes and rolled down her cheek. *Poor fellow*, she thought. *He'll never make it home. If he does, he'll sure be a mess. Not a good sight for anyone to see.*

CHAPTER TWENTY-TWO

WHAT FOLLOWED after that first lucid interval, was a blur to David. The doctors who gave him his first hasty examination in emergency, did their best to make a more thorough examination while they were waiting for passage for him on the ship that was to take the wounded to hospitals in the States, those who were either too seriously wounded to recover enough to return to service or those who required plastic surgery.

David seemed to be in both these categories, for after that first hasty care of his immediate needs, the doctors feared that there might be some internal injuries and possible brain damage, for there was an ugly wound on his head.

He was kept under sedation and was fed through a tube. Those who attended him felt that he had a very slim chance of survival. The nurse who took care of him while he was waiting to be shipped out was hoping that he would recover. Her sympathies were first aroused when he was brought in and after his two buddies had told her what he had done, her admiration for his bravery was added to her sympathy.

She couldn't know that what David had done was not with any consciousness of bravery, only a desire to take revenge in as great a way as possible upon those who had been responsible for Tom's death.

As the hospital ship steamed toward home and safety, David gradually recovered from shock and consciousness returned at brief intervals as the sedative wore off. As the ship drew nearer home, those who were on their way to recovery began to be impatient to see their native land when they had thought that the chances were slim that they ever would.

Those who were too ill or too mutilated, dreaded the prospect of meeting their loved ones when they knew that they were only wrecks with souvenirs of a bestial war that never should have been.

It was early afternoon and a nurse was beside him ready to give him his injection. He opened his eyes slowly, hoping that she would soon be gone and wouldn't linger to try to cheer him up when he didn't want to be cheered. He just wanted to be left alone to bear his physical pain and mental agony.

David pretended to still be asleep, but if she believed that he was asleep, she would stand there and whisper to herself as she had done before when he first came to the receiving station. Telling herself how she pitied him, she wished that she could do something to help him. Once he heard her pray for him.

He felt the slow rolling motion of the ship. He wondered what had happened. It seemed as if the earth was moving, but that couldn't be. It couldn't be the hospital car, for it would be bumping over the rough road, though it traveled slowly.

He opened his eyes, trying to solve the mystery. Then he saw her. His eyes opened wider and he stared at her, trying to remember where he had seen someone who looked like her. It wasn't the young nurse who had first taken care of him. She looked like someone whom he knew. Then he remembered. She looked like Betty, so much like her that he thought his mind was still wandering, for he had been only half conscious, for he didn't know how long. It was uncanny and he stared at her, trying to figure out how two people could look so much alike. He must still be wandering in that half-conscious dream world where he had been ever since that first little while when he had been put in the emergency hospital.

She smiled and spoke and her voice brought him back suddenly into full consciousness with a shock that caused him to utter a gasp.

"David," she said softly, "I'm so thankful that you're so much better. The Lord has surely answered my prayers for you."

She smiled again. He couldn't doubt that voice and he knew that he could never mistake that smile, but it couldn't be. It just couldn't be!

"Betty!" he gasped in a muffled voice through the stiff bandages about his mouth. "It can't be! How! How!"

"It's just one of those miracles that the Lord sometimes performs. A miracle of His love for you and for me."

He tried to say something, but she put out her hand and laid it on his and stopped him.

"Let's not talk about it now. You just lie there quietly and let me give you this little help to keep you quiet and relaxed. We still have quite a while to go before you're safe and comfortable in the hospital at home."

"But I want to know now," he persisted.

She noticed that he didn't stammer and she rejoiced in the evidence of another answer to prayer. She didn't have time to wonder how it happened, she was just glad.

"I'm in the army now," she told him. "It's a long story, but I volunteered for overseas service and they put me on this hospital ship, so here I am. And just in time to be of help to you when you needed me most. Isn't the Lord good?"

He closed his eyes and turned his face away. She could say that, but how could she expect him to agree? Why should he think that the Lord was good to him when He had allowed him to be mutilated as he had been? Where was the Lord when he had stepped on that bomb or whatever it was? It was bad enough when he was as he had been before, but now he would really be a hideous sight to behold. He would have to go off somewhere where he would never have to face people again. Perhaps down in a mine somewhere. What a life that would be! Why didn't God let him be killed out there in that jungle?

Betty saw him close his eyes and turn away and she thought she knew what he was thinking. Her heart went out to him in sympathy and in the love she still had for him. She feared that his heart was so rebellious it would take another miracle from God to enable him to have any love at all for Him when he saw his face after the bandages were removed.

She had seen what was under those bandages and she was shocked by what she saw. It would take a miracle of plastic surgery to repair his face so that it wouldn't be hideous.

She prayed silently for the right words to say. Sympathy wasn't what David needed, for she felt that he had already had too much sympathy and that it had only served to emphasize his despair. She knew his sensitive nature and how he had always felt about himself and she dreaded to think of what would happen when he should see his face and know that he would have to live with it — if he didn't take his life in his despair.

"God was so good to let me be here to be with you and minister to you until you can get those wounds attended to by the most skilled surgeons in our country," she finally said. "I'm so glad, David. Aren't you just a little bit glad that I can minister to you rather than some stranger?"

He turned and looked at her through eyes that were moist.

"I'm glad that you're here," he replied, "but how can you expect me to be glad about anything else? I'll just be glad if God will let me die."

"I pray that He will keep you here, David, until He helps you to get rid of that bitterness. He can help you to believe that He loves you and wants to help you to be happy. Jesus suffered more agony and more mutilation than you could ever have, not because He was defenseless, for He could have called down legions of angels, as He declared, if He had wanted to, but He didn't do that. He suffered and died in order that you might come to God and receive salvation through Him."

"What could anyone do or say to make me want to live? Why should I want to when everyone who sees me will have horror in his eyes? That didn't happen to Jesus, but it has happened to me, so don't try to make me do what I don't feel like doing."

His voice rose in bitterness and again she noticed that he didn't stutter. She would remind him of this later, if he should still need encouragement.

"Do you know what the Bible says about Jesus before He was crucified? He suffered far more mutilation than you have. When those cruel Roman soldiers took Him and beat Him and struck His lovely face and then scourged Him, the Bible says that His face was marred more than the face of any man. And it says, 'We hid our face from him.' The literal meaning of that description is that He had been so brutally mutilated that He scarcely looked like a human being. And He didn't have to submit to that, David. And there was no sedative to ease His pain. He even refused the crude one that was offered to Him, when those other crucified ones took it.

"I think He did that so that those who trust Him, may be sure that He will give comfort and peace to anyone who comes to Him, no matter how deformed or crippled or scarred they may be. He is able and He is willing. It only rests with you or any of those others who may be even worse than you are."

He looked at her and the words came slowly, not because he stammered, but because what she said was stirring something deep within him that he had never experienced before. He was thinking not only of what she was saying, but of what Tom had said so often, that when someone is fully surrendered to the Lord, He gives strength to bear anything that life might bring. He remembered the verse that Tom had so often quoted, "I can do all things through Christ who strengtheneth me."

"I never looked at it like that," he said. "I never knew He looked like that. I thought He was just crucified."

"Just crucified!" she echoed. "Have you ever thought of what that means? Do you realize that that is the most cruel death ever devised by man to torture criminals? The victims often hung there for more than a day, dying by slow torturing minutes. It was agony to have those spikes driven through hands and feet. Just crucified," she repeated. "Perhaps so, but it was for you, so that you might have the strength to bear whatever might come and that you could still rejoice and be glad to be alive."

"But why did I have to come to this?" he persisted. "Wasn't it bad enough before?"

"Remember this, David, and think about it," she said in gentle voice. "When you were out there in that danger zone, you were at enmity with God and consequently you had no right to believe that He would help you. Only when we are in His will can we claim His protection."

"How about my buddy who was killed?" he argued. "Why didn't God save him?"

"I can't answer that. God knows what He's doing and why. Perhaps he was being saved from some great unhappiness that would come to him. I don't know, but he was ready to go. . . . I'm going to leave you now," she said, looking at her watch, "but I'll be back as soon as I'm off duty. Do think about this, David, and don't be so hopeless and so bitter. That will poison your whole life and I know that God has something for you to do or you wouldn't be here now to have another chance. If He hadn't loved you so much, you would never have been spared. I know that both your mother's prayers and mine have been with you and kept you alive until now. Think about it."

She left him and his eyes followed her until she was out of sight along the row of bunks. In his heart there was a strange feeling of shame that he had felt so bitter toward God and His Son. He had been tortured and His face was even worse than his own would be. That was really something to think about.

CHAPTER TWENTY-THREE

DAVID HAD NOTHING TO DO but lie and think and though he tried not to think of what Betty had said, he couldn't stop from thinking about it. The sedatives had been discontinued and he could no longer drift into forgetfulness. His thoughts made him restless and more miserable than ever.

David remembered Betty's words about the crucifixion of Jesus and the torture He had endured before that terrible agony on the cross. He tried not to let his mind dwell upon what she had described from the Bible account of that terrible time, but his mind refused to let him forget. He realized sometimes that he was repeating almost every word that she had used to describe the terrible mutilation of Jesus at the hands of those cruel Roman soldiers.

In the past when his mother had related the story of the crucifixion, she had not dwelt upon the horror and the agony of that time and he had listened indifferently. When she repeated it over and over to him as he grew older, hoping that it might help him yield to the Christ who had given His life for his salvation, he had accepted it as just a story heard too often. Thus he became completely indifferent to the meaning of that story.

He had become like so many others who, refusing to accept what God had for them when He had called to them time after time, became indifferent through a hardening of their heart to the voice of the Holy Spirit.

Memory of Tom came to him and those last whispered words when he seemed to have almost returned from the dead to repeat what he had said so often. And Tom had said he was glad to go. It was because he believed that the life beyond this one was so much more wonderful, that it was not just the mystical dream world so many pictured it, but a life as real as this one, only more wonderful, past man's imagination to conceive.

He wanted to talk to Betty again, yet he dreaded talking to her, for he didn't want any more of her "preaching." He just wanted her nearness and her encouragement, which he needed so terribly.

Presently she came in with the doctor who had given him his first examination when he had been taken aboard. At that time he had been scarcely conscious.

"I think we'll take a look at those upper bandages first," he remarked as he approached David's bunk. "They're not quite as bulky as the others and perhaps we can let him have a little more freedom of movement of his lips."

The bandages were carefully removed while David's eyes were fastened upon the doctor, hoping for some sign as to the extent of the damage. He saw how serious the doctor's face was as he slowly uncovered the mommy-like wrappings and saw the extent of the damage to David's face.

"How bad is it?" David asked fearfully as he saw the doctor's expression.

"Don't talk," the doctor warned. "Not until we get you bound up again. We don't want any of those cuts to be opened up again. It will make it more difficult for the plastic surgeon."

Betty gave him a smile of encouragement. "They look much better than they did when I first saw them," she told him, but her words gave him little comfort.

When the wounds on his body were dressed, they were much more painful than the others had been, but he uttered no sound, just winced when the pain became more severe. When the doctor finished and they turned to leave, David heard him say to Betty, "They're pretty bad. He may always walk with a limp. But those cuts on his face! Poor guy!"

David turned his face to the wall so that no one could see the tears he tried to control.

Betty returned when the doctor had finished his work with the other patients down the line of bunks and pretended that she didn't notice that his eyes were still moist with tears.

"Your wounds are healing nicely," she said encouragingly. "I'm so glad that no infection has set in."

"I heard what the doctor said," he told her. "I'm the poor

guy who's going to be a cripple as well as-as-" and his voice was choked by a sob.

She looked at him for a moment and the expression in her eyes made him turn his face away again. Then she spoke and the tone of her voice made him turn and stare at her in surprise. He had never heard her speak in that tone before.

"David Warner, I'm ashamed of you!" she declared. "You're a coward!"

He gasped in surprise. "Thanks for the compliment," he retorted. His voice was harsh with surprise and pain.

"After such bravery in what you did out there against those snipers, you're just a plain coward. In the heat of battle you could be, oh so brave, but when you have to face the realities of life, that is quite different. You're just plain afraid."

"Wouldn't you be, if you were in my place?" he asked harshly.

"No, I wouldn't be, for I would have Someone who's stronger than I who would give me strength enough not to be afraid."

"Well, I don't have that Someone and I have a right to be afraid of facing the future, so afraid that I don't want to live to face it!"

"Then you'd go out into a Christless eternity and into an existence that would be far more terrible than the life you would face here on earth.

"Would you rather face that than trying to turn your life over to God and trust Him to help you make your life worthwhile? Oh David, why can't you believe that if you'll just trust God to help you live and make your life worth-while, He would do just that? He'd help you to bear whatever the future might hold for you. If you'd only remember those who have gone through life with handicaps and injuries worse than yours and have made the world happier because they have lived in it, you wouldn't be so childishly disconsolate and hopeless. Remember that you no longer stammer. Can you remember what happened? I know that it was of the Lord."

"I remember that I called to the other fellows to follow me when we were out there hunting for those snipers and I didn't even think of stammering. I can't even remember what I said. I know I had to get them into action before more time passed. It was an emergency."

"And you haven't stammered since you came aboard," she added. "One of the men who brought you aboard told me all about that day. He said that sometimes they joked with you about that stammering, but that when you called out those orders to them, he remembered you didn't stammer then. He remarked with a laugh that there was no time to waste with stammering."

"I suppose he was right," David sighed. "I don't remember clearly."

"I believe that God removed that from you when you needed to have your clear speech most. I know that it's gone forever."

"If God did that, then why did He let this happen to me?" he asked.

"I can't answer that," she admitted, "but I know that sometimes God lets a person sink into the depths to make him realize that the only way out is through Him. Perhaps He has done that for you, David."

"Well, I'm down in the depths, all right," he said in somber tones. "I couldn't be any lower and still be alive."

"Then it's time for you to look up, for there's no other way to look. "You've refused to listen to God's call for so many times, that you've become hardened and deaf to the voice of the Holy Spirit. Perhaps God had to do something drastic to make you heed and open your heart to that Voice. He did it in love, not in anger, and perhaps it was the only way your mother's prayers could be answered, for you've refused to listen, so many times, both to her and to me."

He was silent as she prepared to leave. She bent over him and gave him a tender smile and spoke in a low, pleading voice.

"Please believe me that what I've said was in love and friendship and not just to rebuke you. I shall keep on praying also for you and I do beg you to remember that the one way you can still be happy in the life ahead of you is to trust God to give you that happiness and peace."

"I'll try," he said slowly, but he knew that the trying would be almost impossible for him.

When she left he closed his eyes and the tears slipped through the closed lids. *How could I try,* he asked himself, *when I don't even want to begin?*

CHAPTER TWENTY-FOUR

DAVID HAD PLENTY OF TIME TO THINK while the ship drew nearer to America with its cargo of broken bodies and blasted hopes. He saw others who were as completely bandaged as he was, though from much more serious causes. Some had lost legs, while others were blinded.

What he saw and what he heard from the groans of those who were suffering did not add to his own cheerfulness. He tried to forget what he had heard the doctor say about his condition. He must be a terrible sight. And he would not only be that, but he would also be a cripple.

What would his father think of him now, he wondered. He knew that he would be more ashamed of him than he had been before, when he would have a scarred and crippled casualty on his hands.

He tried to forget Betty's words, but they had been burned upon his memory and he couldn't forget them. She had called him a coward and that hurt, though he knew that what she had said was true. He was a coward when it came to facing the future, for he knew how terrible it would be.

She had reminded him that in the midst of battle he had shown such courage that he would receive a medal for his act of bravery, but he knew that this was not the truth and he was ashamed to confess it to himself. There was no bravery in what he did. It was anger and hatred toward the ones who had been responsible for Tom's death. The only emotion that carried him on was the desire to get revenge. It was hatred and murder in his heart, not courage.

During the short time remaining of the voyage, he saw little of Betty. He knew how busy she was, but he hoped that she would at least give him a little time now and then, for he longed for her, even though he knew what she would likely be saying. He didn't know that she was purposely staying away from him. She had said all she could to make him snap out of his gloom. She had prayed for his salvation until she sometimes wondered if David had passed the point of no return, for she remembered that God had said in His Word that "my spirit shall not always strive with man."

She knew also that God had promised to answer the prayer of faith, so she determined to keep on praying for David and believing that her prayers would be answered in God's way and in His time. It was hard to wait and to be patient when she was so eager to see the answer to her prayers, but she remembered that God had said so many times in His Word, "Wait."

It was best to let David have time to think over what she had said, for there was nothing else that she could say.

When at last the ship landed and the wounded were taken to the hospital, David waited impatiently for other news about his condition. He wondered how successful the plastic surgery would be. There was little hope that it would improve his appearance greatly. He remembered the doctor's remark on board the ship.

For a few minutes as he was being taken off to be put in the ambulance waiting at the dock, he saw Betty and talked to her.

"I shall be praying that everything will be done for the best for you and that you will be happier when it's all over," she said as she told him good-by.

There was no time for him to answer and he was glad there wasn't, for there was nothing that he could say that would bring a smile to her face or a more cheerful outlook to his own heart. As the ambulance drove away, he wondered if he would ever see her again. He didn't much care, just then, for he had reached the point long ago where he didn't care much for anything.

His more serious wounds were taken care of first. Some of the minor wounds had already begun to heal, but the deeper jagged cuts were still inflamed and painful, especially one just below the hip that caused pain whenever he moved.

When the doctor had given him a thorough examination, he looked down at David and spoke kindly. He had compassion for the young soldier who had been so brutally injured and he hated to tell him the truth, so he made his remarks as kindly as possible.

"I'm glad to find that you have no internal injuries as far as we can determine and from the reports of your progress on board the ship, I believe that you're well on your way to recovery, though it may be slow. I must be honest and say that I'm afraid the injury to your hip is going to be a little more serious. One of the muscles has been partially severed and it will take some time before you will be able to walk again."

David looked into the kind eyes of the doctor and he knew that the doctor was just trying to make the truth a little easier to bear.

"You're trying to tell me that I'll never walk again," he said.

The doctor smiled and shook his head. "You're just jumping at conclusions. You'll walk again, for which you should be thankful, but you'll have a limp and you may, for a while at least, have to use a cane. In time that muscle may be strong enough to enable you to do without that cane, but you will walk. You should thank the Lord for that."

"Why should I thank the Lord for being a cripple?" David asked bitterly.

"You should be thankful that you didn't lose that leg," the doctor replied while the smile left his lips. "Take a look at that young man across from you. He's lost both legs, but he's thanking God that he's still got his eyesight and his two good arms. You might do well to have his attitude. That young man looks to God for strength to go on, so that's why he can be thankful even in his suffering and injuries. You might look at him and thank God that you got off so well, when you could have been killed, for I'm sure that you were not ready to go."

The doctor left him to his thoughts. David felt ashamed of himself for what he had said. It didn't help him any to express his doubts and voice his bitterness. He'd have to keep them to himself. But the doctor's words kept repeating themselves over and over to him and he grew restless as the pain increased.

After what seemed ages to him in his impatience to hear what the plastic surgeon had to tell him, he finally came. In the meantime he had received letters from his mother and his sister and they both contained messages from his father. He read the letters while he fought back the tears. They didn't know how terribly he had been injured. They had only had a notice that he had been injured and was in the hospital awaiting recovery.

When the bandages were removed from his face and the surgeon examined them carefully, he turned to his assistant without a word to David.

"There is good possibility that we can do something with these cuts, but we can't eliminate them entirely. Fortunately none of them are infected. We'll begin tomorrow. See that he is prepared for the first operation of the morning." Then he left with just a wave of his hand to David.

What a difference between the two doctors, he thought. To one man he was just another case. There seemed to be no real heartfelt interest in him as a human being who might be disfigured for life. To the other, he was a person with heartache and discouragement.

That afternoon when the nurse came with his lunch and she saw his face for the first time without the bandages, she gave a little gasp and he saw the horror in her eyes. He knew what a ghastly sight he must be. Turning his face away, he waved her away.

"But you must eat something," she exclaimed, holding the tray. "You'll need strength for your operation tomorrow."

"What does it matter about that operation?" he cried. "No matter what they try to do, I'll always be someone who'll make people look just as you did when you saw me just now."

"Oh, please don't feel that way!" she exclaimed. "You have no idea what wonderful things Dr. Lawrence can do. You'll be surprised and pleased when you see the result. Please try to eat something."

He shook his head and motioned to her to put the tray down and she left, perturbed because she had betrayed the horror she couldn't conceal.

David turned his face to the wall and covered it with the sheet while he prayed for the first time since he had left his childhood, but his prayer was for death.

"Oh God!" he moaned. "Let me die! Let me die! Anything is better than having to live like this. Let me die. Have mercy and let me die!" Tears flowed and sobs shook him, but in the midst of tears and sobs, there seemed to come a voice that was as distinct as if it had been audible.

"I'm showing mercy by letting you live. If you should die now, where would you be through all eternity?"

He raised his head and looked about fearfully, for he thought surely that voice must have come from someone beside him, but there was no one and he realized that the voice had come from within him. The knowledge frightened and awed him. If God was so near and so powerful that He could speak to his very soul, what could he do or say, but listen? Ashamed of his cowardice, he was sorry for all the long months and the years when he had been deaf to that Voice.

He lay there a moment, stunned and silenced by the revelation of his own stubbornness in refusing to receive what could have been his long ago.

His sobs increased, but he began to speak, though the words were often interrupted by sobs.

"Oh Lord! What can I say? What can I do, but ask for forgiveness for what I've felt toward You for so long? I'm so ashamed! So sorry! Forgive me, Lord, and help me to go on living, even though I know how hard life will be. Please, please forgive me, because Jesus suffered and died for me. I'm sorry, Lord, so sorry!"

Further words were silenced, but the sobs continued for a time until they too grew less and finally stopped. Gradually a strange new peace and calm flooded his being and he seemed to know that all bitterness had been washed out through those tears and the loving mercy of the God whom he had rejected all this long time.

He lay there for a time as he wiped the tears away and murmured a word of humble thanksgiving, relaxed, but exhausted from the emotional battle that had been fought and won by a Power stronger than his.

He fell asleep as he had when he was a child, quietly and no longer filled with turmoil and despair. In his dreams he seemed to see someone beside him, someone who was repeating a verse that he had learned at his mother's knee, but which had long since been forgotten, "Fear not, for I am with thee, be not dismayed for I am thy God. I will comfort thee, I will help thee, I will uphold thee by the right hand of my righteousness."

CHAPTER TWENTY-FIVE

DAVID WAS AWAKENED THE NEXT MORNING by the singing of a bird outside the window of his hospital room. The shrillness of the bird's note penetrated his sleeping and roused him. He lay listening for a little while. It sounded like a mocking bird, but he was not sure that they were found this far away from his southern home.

He smiled, though he didn't know that the smile was a crooked one because of the scars round his mouth. That little bird was doing its utmost to accomplish the thing for which its Maker had fashioned it. Its life was so simple and so short — to sing, to search for food, to find a mate and raise a family. Then when that life was over — nothing.

He thought of his own life and his eyes became clouded. There were many problems facing him, more than he felt capable of handling. Then his eyes became luminous and the cloud faded from them as he remembered the night before. Everything seemed different now. He still grieved over his disfigured face and the lameness that would be with him the rest of his life, but the old bitterness was no longer there. Somehow the dread and the horror of facing the future was gone. He remembered that verse that had come to him and he was humbled and grateful as he felt the beginning of a new peace and strength he had never possessed before. It seemed to pervade his being like some strange elixir or some marvelous sedative that killed fear and brought only peace.

Tears filled his eyes as he realized that it was the peace of God that had entered his being and driven away fear and bitterness, the peace that he had so long refused to accept. He whispered a prayer of thanksgiving for the miracle that had come to him, a miracle far beyond his expectation or power to understand, the miracle that he had believed impossible to him.

128

He knew, and he sighed as the knowledge came to him, that even now it would take more courage than he possessed. It would take a battle which he wasn't able to fight, to go on and try to make the best of a life that wouldn't be easy to live. But now he believed that he would have a strength and a courage outside himself that would enable him to carry on. There would be One with him who had promised never to leave him or forsake him.

When he had finished his whispered prayer and opened his eyes, the little bird had flown away.

He smiled and whispered, "You can go now. I got your message."

When the nurse came with his breakfast he gave her a cheerful good morning which surprised her because there was no scowl upon his face and no gloomy response to her greeting.

"You must be feeling better," she remarked, feeling that he would give his usual reply which was anything but cheerful.

"I am," he said with his crooked smile. "Better on the outside and much better on the inside."

"That's a big help," she replied as she set the tray down and prepared to help him feed himself.

"Let me try," he said. "I'd just as well get used to trying."

"You might hurt that arm," she warned. "It hasn't healed yet."

"I'll be careful. I think I can make it," and he tried to manage, though he winced occasionally from the pain in those muscles that had been injured and were still tender.

"Well," she commented as he continued eating and she saw that she was no longer needed, "I'll say that some miracle must have happened to you. You're not acting like the same person."

He became serious. "A miracle has happened to me. Last night when I had reached the bottom and didn't want to go on any longer, I turned to the Lord and He gave me salvation through the Lord Jesus Christ. I'm really what the Bible calls a new creation in Christ Jesus."

"I'm afraid I don't understand," she murmured, wondering if he was really sane or had suddenly lost his mind.

"I'll try to make you understand," he said as he gave her a smile and finished eating. "When you have time to talk, I'll tell you something about myself and the miracle that came to me last night."

When she returned to the nurse's station she said to the supervisor, "That patient in number sixty has gone haywire. He began quoting the Bible to me and saying that a miracle happened to him last night. Those sedations must have been too strong for him."

When David was taken in for the beginning of his plastic surgery, the doctor tried to encourage him by remarking that the cuts looked much better and that his face would be much improved when he had finally finished his work.

"Don't try to kid me, doctor," David replied. "I've got a pretty good idea what I shall look like, but I'm ready to take whatever happens and make the best of it. I know that the Lord will help me to bear it."

The doctor looked at him skeptically. "I'm glad that you seem to be in a better mood than you were before. That will probably help you to recover more rapidly. The patient's mental attitude has much to do with his recovery, even in plastic surgery."

"Then I'm sure I'll come through with the best results," David said.

The doctor handed David a mirror. David looked at him questioningly.

"I want you to take a look at yourself and see yourself as you are now and take a look after the work is finished. Then you can decide whether it was worth it or not."

David raised the mirror with a shaking hand and took a look at his face. What he saw made him utter a gasp and for a moment the old fear returned. What a horrible mess that explosion had made of his face! How could he ever face life, even if the operation was a success? No operation could take away all those scars.

As he looked at the image in the mirror while fear overwhelmed and despair was taking hold again, gradually that strange new peace entered slowly but surely and he put the mirror down. He now had a God who cared for him enough to have saved his soul. That God could give him strength enough to face whatever the future held and that God could even perform the miracle which seemed so impossible.

He gave the mirror back and remarked, "It's pretty bad, but you just go ahead and do your best. One thing is sure. It can't be any worse than it is now." He tried to smile but the crooked smile was rather feeble.

It was while his wounds were still healing from surgery that he received a notice from the war department stating that his commanding officer had recommended him for a citation for his bravery and that the bronze star together with the purple heart would be presented to him in the near future.

He laid the paper down and turned his face from the young fellow who had brought it. His eyes were moist as he began a whispered prayer.

"Lord," he murmured, "You know that it wasn't bravery that led me to do what I did, but hate, just pure hate. I wanted to kill and kill and kill. Now I believe that You let this terrible thing happen to me to keep me from continuing to have murder in my heart. I know that it was for a purpose and I know that somehow, all things will work for the best in my life. I don't deserve any medal. I don't deserve my salvation, but I thank You for it."

The young fellow still stood there wondering at his strange behavior. He saw the notice and knew what it contained.

"You should be very proud of this honor, sir," he remarked. "I know I would be."

"Thanks, fellow," David replied and gave him a smile.

When the young man left. David lay there thinking. He knew that it would take more courage than he now possessed to face even a small group that might be there when he received his honors. It would take even more courage to face those at home who didn't yet know the damage he had received. But he knew that prayer would help him to have that courage when the time came. He glanced at the notice once more, then laid it on the stand nearby and closed his eyes.

When the doctor came in and saw the notice lying beside the bed while David was fast asleep, he smiled as he looked down at his sleeping patient.

"You surely took this calmly. You're a conundrum. I wonder what happened to you to change you almost overnight from a cringing, miserably unhappy person to what you seem to be now."

Since David couldn't hear that remark, the doctor received no answer and the conundrum was not solved. Not for the present at least.

CHAPTER TWENTY-SIX

DAVID WAS AT LAST ON HIS WAY HOME and mingled emotions whirled through him as he sat looking out of the window of the plane, yet not observing the beautiful cloud formations around and below him. He was excited and happy at the thought of being home again when he'd had no hope of ever seeing it.

He was apprehensive and a little bit worried as he felt his face and realized that the marks of his injuries had not been entirely obliterated in spite of the skill of the surgeon. But his thoughts didn't linger long on those scars, for he was thinking of how his mother would rejoice when he told her that her prayers had at last been answered and that he was now really a new creation in Christ Jesus. He had purposely kept the news from her, for he wanted the joy of telling her when he could see the joy on her face.

Even yet they didn't know the real nature of his injuries and he knew that it would be a shock to them when they saw him. He dreaded that ordeal, but he knew that he would have the courage to face it when it came.

David wouldn't let his thoughts dwell upon his father. He had prayed about his father and he no longer felt the old bitterness toward him, but he knew that it would take time and the grace of God for him to have a real love for him.

He wondered where Betty was, though he knew that the ship was somewhere on its way to convey the injured home. He longed to be able to tell her that at last her prayers also had been answered. He didn't want to write the good news, though he knew that there was little chance that he would be able to tell her in person.

There had been a little ceremony in the hospital when a representative from his general had pinned his decorations upon him — the bronze star and the purple heart with one leaf.

He felt guilty during the short speech, for he felt that he didn't deserve those honors. He remembered the spirit that had motivated his actions. It was hatred, vengeance, and murder that had spurred him on, not bravery to win a battle.

He had not told his mother about those decorations, partly for the same reason. He wanted to tell her when they were alone and he could pour out his heart to her as he could do to no one else but God.

What he didn't know was that the news of his citation had been in the hometown paper, together with a photograph of himself and the others there in the hospital. When he came down the ramp at the airport and saw the group waiting there, he thought they must be waiting to greet someone of importance, for he only glanced casually at the group. He was anxious to see his mother whom he felt sure would be there. When he left the ramp, still not noticing the group, but looking for his mother, he saw her in their midst. Forgetting the crowd, he went to her as she held out her arms to him. While he put his arms around her and their lips met, the group started clapping and he was overwhelmed when he realized that they had come to meet him.

He was led to the car where his sister sat waiting to welcome him. His mother told him that his father had been delayed, but that he would be at the church to meet them.

"At the church?" David asked in surprise. "What's going on there?"

"A little celebration for our returning hero," she told him. "Don't you realize that you are our first returned hero from the war? It was in our paper, all about you and that little ceremony in the hospital. One of the men there took the picture and sent it to our paper. Now our church people and some of the other citizens are waiting to show you how proud we all are of you."

"Oh my!" David breathed as he ran his fingers over those lines on his face.

"Don't worry about them, dear," his mother said. "They're not bad at all." Then she suddenly realized something. "David! You don't stammer any more. What happened? How did you get cured?"

He smiled. "I suppose it must have been shock. When we were cut off from the others and there was no one else to give orders to go ahead and get revenge on those demons, I just shouted to them to come on with me. I guess I forgot to stammer. I didn't have time to do that," he added with a little laugh.

When they reached the church David saw that it was packed. He felt panic coming on and he uttered a quick, desperate, whispered prayer that he would know what to do and say. Escorted to the front of the church, he saw his father seated and he sat down beside him. He noticed a smile upon his father's face and a light in his eyes that he had never seen there before. There was sudden moisture in his eyes as he saw that look and he returned his father's smile.

After a hymn and a short prayer by the pastor, one of the deacons came forward and began an introduction of David. He told them how proud they were that one of their citizens had won such honors and they rejoiced to give him this little evidence of their pride in him. Then he asked David to come to the platform and tell them something of what had happened when he had displayed the courage that had won those decorations.

David hesitated a moment before he rose and he uttered another prayer that the Lord would put words in his mouth, for he felt utterly inadequate to meet the situation.

His face was grave as he walked slowly, still carrying the cane he had to use and mounted the steps and stood beside the speaker. As he faced the crowd, all his nervousness vanished and he felt a calmness that he had not felt a few moments before. And in that moment, he forgot all about the lines upon his face or what the audience might be thinking as they beheld them.

Those who had known him better, were puzzled as they looked at him. Those lines upon his face gave his face a certain character that it had not possessed before. They had, in a way, transformed his face. It was no longer a caricature, with features out of proportion. It was not handsome, but there was a certain attractiveness that it had never possessed before. The plastic surgeon had unwittingly accomplished this. There was something else, however, that made his acquaintances observe him closely. There was a different expression upon David's face. They had only known him with that sullen and unhappy expression that he had always worn.

He smiled as he stood there for a moment before he attempted to speak. Those who knew him best were surprised even more when he smiled. That smile transformed his face and gave a light to his eyes, the most attractive feature he possessed.

When he began to speak, slowly, but with firm voice while the smile still remained, they were astonished and some of them looked at each other in amazement. He no longer stammered!

"I appreciate what you are doing for me, far more than I can tell you," he began, "but it's such an overwhelming surprise that I find myself at a loss what to say. I had thought that I'd slip home quietly and have a happy homecoming with my family, but it seems that you are giving me something other than that.

"I don't want to weary you by giving you an account of my life in the army, for I know that you have heard enough of that already and you have perhaps heard exaggerated accounts of what happened while I was in battle.

"What I would like to tell you is about something that happened to me when I was in the hospital. It was far more important to me than any medal I could ever receive or any honor that could be bestowed on me.

"When I was recovering from the wounds that not only disfigured my face more than ever, but which left me a cripple, I didn't want to live. I didn't want to face the future, being what I had become. Life was hard enough for me before.

"All my life I had heard my mother pleading with me to accept Christ as my Saviour, but bitterness filled me so that I didn't want to yield my life to God. In fact I was bitter toward God for making me as unattractive as I was and the handicap that I possessed. Those of you who knew me best, know that I stammered and that gave me such an inferiority complex that I became silent and moody and wouldn't even try to make friends.

"There was a friend, though, who just wouldn't give me up. When others scorned me and spurned me, she clung to me in the greatest friendship that a fellow could ever hope to have. She tried to give me hope to struggle on, in spite of my every handicap, but I wouldn't yield to her pleas, for bitterness filled my soul. But when I went down into the depths after that explosion that left me as I am now and when I had nowhere else to go I turned at last to God and I asked Him to forgive me and save my poor unworthy soul. And He did just that.

"There was a song that I heard and that I loved so that I learned the words long ago. Somehow that song awakened a longing within me, though it caused such unrest and unhappiness when I heard the words. That song is "OVERSHADOWED." This friend sang it for me one day when I was down in the depths and though I didn't believe that I could ever be overshadowed by God's love, I loved the song and I've always remembered it as she sang it that day, without any accompaniment, just sitting on a bench under a tree.

"Now that I've learned what a blessing it is to know that I am overshadowed by God's mighty love, I would be so glad to tell her, as I am now telling my dear mother, how I thank her for those prayers that she never ceased to utter for my salvation. From now on, my whole desire in life shall be to live so that I may be pleasing to the Lord who has overshadowed me with His love, when I so rebelliously refused to accept that love.

"I thank you for your patience in listening to me and I do appreciate more than words can tell, what you have done for me tonight. I'm grateful, though I know that I don't deserve this honor, nor do I deserve the salvation that was so freely given to me."

Before David could move to leave the platform and before anyone could stir, someone struck a chord on the piano and a voice rang out sweet and clear singing the words, "Overshadowed by His mighty love," and on to the end of that lovely song.

David stood transfixed. He knew that voice, though he hadn't seen her hidden behind the piano. As he turned to look, no one else moved until the song was finished. He saw also the light in her eyes as their eyes met and his heart was thrilled with a strange new emotion. Then he knew. He knew a truth that he should have known long ago. It was not friendship that he felt for Betty, but a love so overwhelming that it startled him, because he had been blind to it for so long.

He stood now looking at her, forgetful of the crowd, the watching eyes, forgetful of the fact that the pastor had risen and was standing beside him waiting to pronounce the benediction.

When the song had ended on the last clear note, the pastor uttered a short prayer, then led David down so that those who came forward could shake hands with him. He responded to the greetings of the many who came to him, but his thoughts were not on what they were saying. He was looking at Betty. She was standing beside the piano in the background, looking at him with shining eyes. He was impatient to get away from the crowd and get to her. What a poor blind idiot he had been all this long while, not to have known the truth!

CHAPTER TWENTY-SEVEN

ONLY A FEW PEOPLE REMAINED. They were the ones who had known his family the best. Thrilled at the change they saw in him, they were rejoicing over his testimony and wanted to linger and talk with him. He tried to be polite and listen to their remarks, but he was so impatient to get to Betty that he found it difficult to appear interested. While he appreciated their interest, there was something more important to him just then than anything else.

As the last ones were leaving, he saw Janice coming toward him. She had waited until the others had left. The sight of her gave him a shock. He had forgotten her completely! A great wave of thanksgiving swept through him as the revelation came to him. Even the memory of the many hours of longing and mingled love and hatred that he had experienced, were forgotten.

Janice extended her hand and her eyes were pleading as she spoke.

"I'm so glad to see you again and so proud of you, David. You look simply wonderful," she added while she smiled her usual charming smile.

He received another shock — he had forgotten his looks entirely! In the back of his consciousness, he remembered that not one of those who had talked with him had looked at him with pity or revulsion, as he had seen so often in the past. Another great wave of thankfulness spread through him. He was free at last from that terrible self-consciousness. From now on he would never let the thought of his appearance bother him. He would make the best of what he had and thank God for it and live to keep the inner self beautiful and acceptable in His sight.

"Thank you," he said politely. "I really feel wonderful. I have so much to thank the Lord for."

He wasn't looking at her, but over at Betty and he gave her a smile. Janice saw the look he gave Betty and she saw Betty's answering smile. That nettled her, but she still pursued her effort to restore what she had lost, for she felt that she had lost.

"David, I do hope that we can still be friends, that you will forgive me and try to forget," she said in her most persuasive voice.

"Just forget it," he advised, still looking at Betty. "Don't let it bother you," and he waved his hand toward her and crossed to where Betty was standing.

Janice's lip tightened and she turned away feeling angry at being rebuffed.

David took Betty's hand in both of his and exclaimed, "What a wonderful end to such a wonderful day to see you and to hear you sing that song! I shall remember that as long as I live. I thought you were on the high seas somewhere. When may I see you, so that we can talk? I have so much to tell you."

"Come over later this evening," she suggested. "I'm anxious to hear everything that happened since you left the ship."

"I'll be over right after dinner," he told her.

Just then he saw his father approaching.

"Let's go, son. Your mother is waiting for us in the car."

They told Betty good-by and left her. David sat beside his mother, while his sister sat beside his father in front.

"There's no need for me to tell you how happy I am over the answer to my prayers," his mother began. "I couldn't stay there in the church, because I knew I would cry, so I came out here where I could shed those tears of joy in private."

"Bless you, Mom. I wanted you to be the first one to know, but it just happened to turn out differently."

When they reached home, his mother and sister left him with his father. His mother knew that his father wanted to talk to David. As soon as they were alone, his father sat down beside him.

"I don't know whether you can ever forgive me, my son," he began, "for the attitude I've had toward you all these years. I'm sure that you sensed it, even when you were very young. I seemed to know that you feared me and I didn't do anything to change your feeling, for I just didn't care."

"I didn't fear you, Dad, but I was bitter because I knew how you felt toward me. I couldn't understand it when I was a little fellow, but it made me afraid of you. I knew the reason when I overheard you and mother talking about me once when she was rebuking you for being so harsh with me. From then on, perhaps I did have hatred in my heart, though I couldn't understand the emotion then. I longed to be loved and it seemed that no one loved me but Mother."

His father bowed his head at David's confession, then he raised it and looked at his son through moist eyes.

"I don't know how God could forgive me for being such a sinner, but He did," and his voice broke. "Then I realized how terrible I had been and how cruel to you, because you were not just what I had expected in a son."

"I can understand that now, but then it was the bitterness that filled my life and that made me refuse to listen to anything that Mom had to say, when she talked to me about the love of God. I felt that God felt the same way about me that you did, yet it was He who had made me what I was."

"We both have much to thank God for," his father said. "Perhaps you don't realize all that happened to you upon that battleground. It not only brought you face to face with God and His salvation, but those very scars which caused you so much agony in the beginning have been a blessing in a strange way. But it was not so strange, after all, for I know it was of God that it happened as it did. Those scars have changed your face in a wonderful way. You're not handsome, but you have a certain attractiveness that I can't explain. The lines show, but they somehow give your face a character that it never had before. But that isn't what is the most important. It's what God has put inside of you that makes the difference in you and it's what He has put inside of me that makes me feel so different toward you and so ashamed of how I denied you all these years. Can you ever forgive me?" His voice shook with emotion.

"Of course I can, Dad, and I do." His own eyes filled with tears. They both rose and as if at a signal they were in each other's arms and their tears mingled as the older man put his cheek against David's.

When they both joined David's mother and sister, they knew that at last there was love and companionship between them and there was a time of rejoicing among them.

Later David hurried over to see Betty. She greeted him with the smile he loved and led him into the living room.

When they were seated, she said, "Now tell me everything. I'm so eager to hear it all."

"Tell me first, had you planned to sing that song before I came?"

"No, for I had no idea what you were going to say, but when you said what you did about the song, I just felt I had to sing it and I did it on pure impulse. I never thought that perhaps I shouldn't have done it."

"As far as I'm concerned, it was the best thing you ever did in your life, for it made me realize what an utter fool I had been all this long time."

"I'm glad that if any little word of mine or any act has helped you in any way," she said quietly. She thought that he was talking of his salvation, yet she couldn't quite understand just why he made that statement if it referred to his salvation.

"I'm not talking about my salvation, Betty. I'm talking of something quite different, though I know that it was your influence and your words of pleading as well as warning that helped, even more than my mother's, to bring me to that final surrender. You were the only real friend I had beside her and I longed for you and your comfort even though I refused to do what you so longed for me to do. But that's not what I'm talking about now. When you sang that song this afternoon, I knew that I had to tell you what it did to me, even though you might not be pleased when I tell it.

"I just want to tell you, Betty darling, that I love you with all the love of my heart, with a love that I never thought possible for anyone. I knew it when you sang. I knew that it wasn't friendship that I had for you all this time, but a love that I was too stupid to see. I'm not even hoping that you could love me, that you could give your life to a cripple like me with a face like mine, but I beg you to continue to be my friend and give me the joy of having your friendship. Just knowing that you still care as a friend will help me to keep on going when I shall be lonely and will need a friend."

She was silent for a moment, then she gave him a smile as she placed her hand upon his.

"You're a stupid man, David. Only a person as stupid as you are could have been with me all those past months and not have guessed that I was trying so hard to keep my love for you from showing."

His mouth flew open and he stared at her with such a surprised expression that she laughed a happy little laugh.

"How could that be?" he asked, wondering if he had really heard rightly.

"I don't know, David dear," she said in tender tones. "I asked myself many times how it could be, but I don't know. It was of God. You see, He had you picked out for me and He had me chosen for you, though we had no idea of it. I do love you, David, but not as a friend. I've loved you for so long. Perhaps that is why I prayed so earnestly for your salvation."

"Do you mean that you'd be willing to marry me? Me, a cripple with a scarred face?" He was still unable to believe it was true.

"I mean that I shall be glad to marry you. You're not a cripple, but I'd marry you if you were. And your face is beautiful to me, for now that you have those scars, somehow it has character. I don't know how that change came about, but I believe that it was of God."

He took her in his arms. His lips met hers and her kiss answered his. He held her close for a moment, then he asked, "How soon will you marry me?"

"As soon as I get my discharge. That will be in a few months. And when you are settled in what you want to do," she added.

"I haven't thought much about that," he admitted. "I suppose I'll try to go back to my job, but I want to do what the Lord would have me do."

"How about getting that voice trained while you're waiting for me to get my discharge?" she suggested. "Then, if the Lord should call us for work for Him, both of us would be prepared to help with music that is so important in His work."

"I'll do that," he agreed. "But all that I want to know now is that I have you and that you want me and that we shall have each other as long as life lasts. Isn't life wonderful?" he cried. "How good it is to be alive!"

"Do you know that's the first time I ever heard you say that?" she asked.

"I believe it's the first time I've ever said it," he replied with a little laugh, "but it's the first time I've ever had so much to live for."

"Let's pray that we shall always be able to say that," she suggested.

"I shall be able to say that as long as I have you," he said. They bowed their heads and prayed silently that they would live for God together.